Sophie's First Dance

Other books in the growing Faithgirlz!™ library

The Faithgirlz!™ Bible
Faithgirlz!™ Backpack Bible
My Faithgirlz!™ Journal

The Sophie Series

Sophie's World (Book One)
Sophie's Secret (Book Two)
Sophie Under Pressure (Book Three)
Sophie Steps Up (Book Four)
Sophie's Stormy Summer (Book Six)
Sophie's Friendship Fiasco (Book Seven)
Sophie and the New Girl (Book Eight)
Sophie Flakes Out (Book Nine)
Sophie Loves Jimmy (Book Ten)
Sophie's Drama (Book Eleven)
Sophie Gets Real (Book Twelve)

Nonfiction

Body Talk
Beauty Lab
Everybody Tells Me to Be Myself but I Don't Know Who I Am
Girl Politics

Check out www.faithgirlz.com

SOPHIE'S
First Dance

5

Nancy Rue

ZONDERVAN.com/
AUTHORTRACKER
follow your favorite authors

ZONDERKIDZ

Sophie's First Dance
Copyright © 2005, 2009 by Nancy Rue

Requests for information should be addressed to:

Zondervan, *Grand Rapids, Michigan* 49530

Library of Congress Cataloging-in-Publication Data

Rue, Nancy N.
    Sophie's first dance / Nancy Rue. – 1st ed.
        p. cm. – (Faithgirlz)
    Summary: As the sixth-grade dance approaches, Sophie turns to Dr. Peter and Jesus for help while trying to cope with her new feelings towards boys and with new tensions within her group of friends, the Corn Flakes.
    ISBN: 978-0-310-70760-8 (softcover)
    [1. Friendship – Fiction. 2. Interpersonal relations – Fiction. 3. Imagination – Fiction. 4. Schools – Fiction. 5. Christian life – Fiction. 6. Virginia – Fiction.] I. Title. II. Series.
PZ7.R88515Sk 2005
[Fic] – dc22

                              2004029451

Published in association with the literary agency of Alive Communications, Inc., 7680 Goddard Street, Suite 200, Colorado Springs, CO 80920. www.alivecommunucations.com

Zonderkidz is a trademark of Zondervan.

Interior art direction and design: Sarah Molegraaf
Cover illustrator: Steve James
Interior design and composition: Carlos Estrada and Sherri L. Hoffman

Printed in the United States of America

---

11 12 13 14 15 16 /DCI/ 33 32 31 30 29 28 27 26 25 24 23 22 21 20 19 18 17 16 15 14 13 12

So we fix our eyes not on what is seen,
but on what is unseen.
For what is seen is temporary,
but what is unseen is eternal.

—2 CORINTHIANS 4:18

One

Are you going to feed us something weird for your report?"

Sophie LaCroix looked up from the library table into the disdainful face of B.J. Schneider. *Disdainful* was a word Sophie's best friend, Fiona, had taught her, and this word definitely worked when B.J. or one of the other Corn Pops narrowed her eyes into slits, curled her lip, and acted as if Sophie were barely worth the breath it was taking to say something heinous to her.

"As a matter of fact, yes," that same Fiona said as she tucked a strand of dark hair behind her ear. It popped back out and draped over one gray eye. "We thought we'd dish up some sautéed roaches on a bed of seaweed with a nice snake venom sauce."

Sophie dragged a piece of her own hair under her nose like a mustache.

"It is so disgusting when you do that," said another Corn Pop, Anne-Stuart—with the usual juicy sniff up her nostrils.

Not as disgusting as you and your sinus problems, Sophie thought. But she didn't say it. All of the Corn Flakes had taken a vow not to be hateful to the Corn Pops ever, no matter how heinous THEY were to the Flakes.

B.J. put her hands on her slightly pudgy hips. "I KNOW you aren't really going to serve something that nasty for your culture project," she said.

Fiona pulled her bow of a mouth into a sly smile. "Then why did you ask?"

B.J. and Anne-Stuart rolled their eyes with the precision of synchronized swimmers.

"What are y'all doing for your presentation?" Sophie said, adjusting her glasses on her nose.

"We AND Julia and Willoughby—we're doing a folk dance," Anne-Stuart said. "And we're going to make the whole class participate."

"You're going to 'make' us?" Fiona said.

Sophie cleared her throat. Sometimes Fiona had a little trouble keeping the vow. It *was* hard with the Corn Pops acting like they ran Great Marsh Elementary, especially when school stretched into Saturdays at the town library.

"Then everybody can get used to dancing with each other," Anne-Stuart said. She sniffled. "That way, SOME people won't feel so lame at the graduation dance."

"What graduation dance?" Sophie and Fiona said together. Sophie's voice squeaked higher than Fiona's, which brought a heavy-eyebrowed look from the librarian.

"What dance?" Fiona said again.

B.J. and Anne-Stuart both sat down at the table with Sophie and Fiona—as if they'd been invited—and B.J. shoved aside the *Food from Around the World* book they'd been looking at while Anne-Stuart leaned in her long, lean frame. Sophie was sure she could see moisture glistening on Anne-Stuart's nose hairs.

"The dance the school is having at the end of the year for our sixth-grade graduation," she said.

"Duh," B.J. put in.

"Who decided that?" Fiona said.

"Just the entire class. Back in September." B.J. gave her buttery-blonde bob a toss. "You were probably off in one of those weird things y'all do—making up stories—"

"No," Fiona said. "I wasn't even HERE yet in September. I moved here in October."

"I know YOU were here," Anne-Stuart said, pointing at Sophie.

Sophie shrugged. She knew she had probably daydreamed her way through the entire voting process. That was back before she'd gotten her video camera, and before she and the Corn Flakes had started making films out of their daydreams instead of getting in trouble for having them in school and missing important things like voting for a stupid dance.

"What were the other choices?" Fiona said.

"Who cares?" B.J. said. "We're having a dance, and everybody's going to wear, like, dress-up clothes, and—"

"So if you didn't even know about the dance," Anne-Stuart said, "then you obviously don't have your dates yet."

"Dates?" Sophie said.

"You mean, as in boys?" Fiona said.

Anne-Stuart snorted and covered her mouth. B.J. waved at the librarian, whose eyebrows were now up in her hairline.

"You know," Anne-Stuart whispered. "Boys. The ones with the cute legs."

"Cute LEGS?" Sophie's voice squeaked out of her own nostrils, and she was sure Anne-Stuart was going to drip right out of her chair. B.J. kept smiling at the librarian.

"People are actually coming to the dance with DATES?" Fiona said.

"You meet your date at the dance, and he doesn't dance with anybody else but you the whole night." Anne-Stuart put her hand on Fiona's and wrinkled her forehead. "You don't HAVE to. I mean, if you can't get a boy to be with you, then you can't."

"I don't WANT a boy to be with me, thank you very much," Fiona said. She snatched back her hand.

Sophie was doing the mustache thing with her hair again. What boy in their class would she even want to get within three feet of? One of the Fruit Loops—Tod or Eddie or Colton? The thought made her feel like she had the stomach flu coming on. She shrank her already tiny form down into the chair.

Tod Ravelli had a pointy face like a Dr. Seuss character and acted like he was all big, even though he was one of the shrimpiest boys in the class. Acting big included trying to make Sophie feel like a worm.

Colton Messik wasn't any better. He seemed to think he was cute the way he could make the Corn Pops squeal when he told a joke. Sophie and the rest of the Flakes thought the only thing funny about him was the way his ears stuck out.

And Eddie Wornom was the worst. He acted like Mr. Football, but mostly he was what Sophie's mom called "fluffy" around the tummy, and he was louder than the other two put together, especially when he was calling their friend Maggie "Maggot" or some other lovely thing.

"I doubt any boy would ask you anyway," B.J was saying to Fiona. "Not unless it was one of the computer geeks. Vincent or one of the boy-twins or—I know! Jimmy Wythe—he's like the KING of the computer geeks. You could go with him."

Fiona let her head fall to the side, closed her eyes, and pretended to snore. Sophie watched the librarian march toward them. B.J. lowered her voice. "But you'd better hurry up because there are more girls than boys in our class. You COULD get left out."

"We have to go," Anne-Stuart said. She grabbed B.J.'s hand, pulling her from the chair, and cocked her head at Mrs. Eyebrows. Silky-blonde tresses spilled along the side of Anne-Stuart's face.

"We tried to get them to be quiet, ma'am," she said. She and B.J. trailed off.

"Come on," Fiona said. "Let's wait for Kitty and those guys outside."

Sophie left *Food from Around the World* on the table and followed Fiona past the glowering Mrs. Eyebrows and on outside—where a corridor of trees sheltered the library and Poquoson, Virginia's City Hall from the road. Big, fluffy hydrangea bushes provided a getaway spot for the two of them. Sophie sat down on the curb and wriggled herself under a snowball cluster of blue flowers with Fiona perched next to her.

"Just when I think they couldn't GET any more scornful, they reveal yet another layer of contempt—" Fiona's eyes narrowed, Corn Pop style. "They're evil."

Sophie nodded. "And Julia wasn't even with them. Or Willoughby."

"Julia always lets them do the dirty work, being the queen and all. And Willoughby—you can hardly tell if she's even a Corn Pop anymore. Have you noticed that sometimes she's with them and sometimes she's not?"

"I invited her to hang out with us that one time—"

"And the Pops snatched her right back. Even if THEY don't want to be her friends, they don't want US to be her friends. I told you—they're evil."

Sophie squirmed. "What about this dance thing?"

"It's lame. I vote the Corn Flakes just don't even go. We have better things to do. Hey—I have an idea." Fiona nodded toward Sophie's backpack. "Get your camera out. Let's hide in this bush and film Kitty and Darbie and Maggie when they get here."

Sophie felt a grin spreading across her face. "Let's pretend we're secret agents—"

"Hired to do surveillance on—"

"A new group of agents being gathered for a special mission—"

"Quick—here comes Maggie's mom's car!"

As Senora LaQuita's big old Pontiac pulled into the parking lot, Sophie climbed into the hydrangea bush with Fiona, fished the camera out of her backpack, and became—

Agent Shadow. With a practiced hand—and eye—Agent Shadow framed her fellow agent in the lens. Wide-set brown eyes, dark chin-length hair, and a classic jaw line revealed her Latino heritage. An experienced agent knew these things. The dark-haired agent didn't say goodbye as she drew her boxy-square frame from the car, but, then, according to classified information, this was not a smiley spy. Agent-from-Cuba was known as the most serious of this collection of agents from all over the world.

Yeah—an international group. That was good, Sophie decided.

As Maggie plodded up the library walk with her leather backpack, Sophie panned the camera, but Fiona gave her a poke and pointed back to the parking lot. A van was pulling up.

"There's Kitty," Sophie whispered to Fiona.

Agent Shadow focused the camera and watched the girl hop down from the van, her black ponytail bouncing. Agent Shadow continued to film Agent Ponytail as she stood on tiptoe to talk through the window to the driver. Agent Shadow was sure Ponytail was getting ALL the instructions about when to be back at headquarters—for the fourth time at least. This agent's documents had revealed that she could be scatterbrained at times. Just as Ponytail turned, Agent Shadow got a good shot of her profile—an upturned nose that looked like it had been chiseled out of china. Agent Ponytail was very un-agent-like. That must be part of her cover.

"Hey, Mags!" Kitty called up the walk.

Agent Shadow jumped and collided with Agent Big Words, nearly tumbling the two of them from their hiding place—

"Better let me," Fiona said. She picked up the camera from where it teetered on a hydrangea branch.

Agent Shadow grew more intent as she crept deeper under cover. She had been in the field for forty-eight straight hours without sleep. Perhaps it was time to let Agent Big Words take over the filming.

She watched, her mind razor-sharp, as Agent Ponytail hugged the neck of Agent-from-Cuba. Agent Ponytail appeared to be the slobbery type. Agent-from-Cuba obviously was not.

"Psst—here comes Darbie!" Fiona hissed.

Agent Shadow swiveled her gaze to the figure getting out of a BMW. She was the newest agent to be recruited into this gathering. Recently arriving from Northern Ireland, she would have much to add to the mission internationally speaking, especially when Agent Shadow determined just what the mission was—which would come later. It always came later.

Refreshed from her short break from the camera, Agent Shadow snatched it back from Agent Big Words and zoomed in on the subject striding up the walk. She was swinging her arms and her reddish hair and taking in everything with flashing black eyes.

"Agent Irish will be helpful in giving each of our agents new names and identities," *Agent Shadow told herself.* "Once we figure out what dangerous, risky, and utterly vital mission we'll be on. But first I must see just how observant she is. Can we remain hidden—or is she just as sharp as her file says she is?"

Even though Agent Shadow burrowed herself deeper into the treacherous tangle of brush, she could see Agent Irish growing bigger in her lens—and bigger—and bigger—

"Don't be thinking you're sly, you two," Darbie said, her nose pressed against the camera lens. "You're just a bit obvious."

"But we got you on film!" Fiona said. She crawled from behind the bush, shaking tiny blue blossoms from her hair. Sophie wriggled out after her.

"Our next Corn Flakes production should be a spy film, I think," Sophie said.

"My mom could make us trench coats," Maggie said.

Fiona bunched up her lips. "That's better than dance dresses."

"DANCE dresses?" Kitty's clear blue eyes were lighting up like tiny flames. "That's right—the sixth-grade dance!"

"You knew about it?" Fiona said.

"Of course she did. So did I." Maggie shrugged. "They do it every year."

Darbie gave a grunt. "You won't be seeing me at a dance. Those Corn Pops already made me feel like an eejit about my dancing when I first came here." *Eejit* was *idiot* in Darbie's Northern Irish accent. It was one of her favorite words. "I'd rather be making a spy flick," she said.

"Exactly," Fiona said.

Sophie looked at Kitty, who was poking at a weed growing up through a walkway crack with the toe of her pink flip-flop.

"You WANT to go to the dance, Kitty?" Sophie said.

"Kind of," Kitty said. "It would be fun to be all, like, dressed up. We don't HAVE to dance." Kitty's voice was starting to spiral up into a whine. Whining was one of the things she did best.

"You just want to get dressed up and go stand around?" Fiona said.

"Maybe we could just dance with each another—"

"And pretend we're agents in disguise, keeping the Corn Pop organization in our sights," Sophie said.

"That definitely has possibilities," Fiona said, rubbing her chin. "What if we could foil their plans with their 'dates'?"

"Define 'foil'" Darbie said.

"I think that means mess them up," Sophie said.

Darbie giggled. "You mean, like mix them up so they end up dancing with each other's boyfriends?" she said.

"The only thing is," Sophie said, "we can't be hateful to the Pops just because they're hateful to us. Corn Flake code."

"I know—bummer," Fiona said. She sighed. "But you're right. We'll have to think of some other mission."

"Whatever it is, we can't let them see us filming them," Darbie put in.

"WE don't have to dance with any boys though, do we?" Maggie's voice was thudding even harder than usual.

"Absolutely not," Darbie said. "We'll have nothing to do with those blaggards."

Blaggards, Sophie thought, repeating the word *blackguards* in her mind the way Darbie had pronounced it. With her Irish accent, Darbie could make anything sound exciting and exotic and worth doing.

"We might look a little suspicious not dancing with ANY boys," Kitty said. "It's not like ALL of them are blackguards."

"The Fruit Loops definitely are," Fiona said with a sniff. She dropped down on the grass and the rest of the Corn Flakes joined her.

Darbie nodded slowly. "But those boys that are always raving on about computers—they aren't THAT bad."

"You mean like Nathan and Vincent and Jimmy and the twins?" Sophie said.

"Ross and Ian," Kitty said.

Sophie peered at Kitty through her glasses. Kitty was looking suspiciously dreamy, and Sophie had a feeling it wasn't about being a secret agent.

"I can't keep any of them straight," Darbie said.

"Nathan's way skinny and he got first place in the science fair, remember?" Kitty said.

"No," Fiona said. "Why do you remember?"

Kitty's cheeks got pink. "His dad's in my dad's squadron. I see him at picnics and stuff."

"Carry on," Darbie said, pointing at Kitty with a piece of grass.

"Like I said, Ross and Ian are the twins—"

"Round faces," Maggie said.

"Not Eddie Wornom-round, though," Sophie said.

"No—eew," Kitty said. "What else, Darbie?" Her eyes were shining, and Sophie could tell she was enjoying this role.

This might come in handy when we make our secret agent movie, Sophie thought. She was already thinking of plot twists that could make use of Agent Ponytail's powers of observation.

"Vincent—which one is he?"

"Curly hair, braces," Fiona said.

"And he has kind of a deep voice," Kitty cut in—before Fiona could take her job away from her, Sophie thought. "Only it goes high sometimes."

"I know exactly who he is," Darbie said. "He isn't as much of an eejit as a lot of them."

"You left out Jimmy Wythe," Maggie said matter-of-factly.

Kitty shrugged. "I don't know that much about him. He's quiet." She gave a soft giggle. "That kind of makes him mysterious."

"Or a geek," Fiona said.

"Okay," Sophie said. "So when we come up with a mission, if we have to dance with any boys it'll be just those not-mean ones. Is everybody in?"

Fiona stuck out her pinky finger, and Kitty latched onto it. Maggie hooked onto Kitty's, and Sophie crooked her pinky around Maggie's. Only Darbie was left.

"Are we promising there will be no dates for us though?" she said.

"Not a chance," Fiona said.

Darbie gave a serious nod, and then she curved one pinky around Sophie's and the other around Fiona's.

"It's a Corn Flakes pact then," Fiona said. "No one breaks it."

"We better get to work on our culture project now," Maggie said.

Kitty giggled and hiked herself up onto Maggie's back, right on top of her backpack. "Can't we talk about our dresses first?" she said.

"Costumes," Sophie said. "For the film."

As the Corn Flakes meandered toward the library door, Sophie held back. She had a feeling this was going to be the Corn Flakes' most important movie yet—and maybe even Agent Shadow's most important mission. It was going to take some serious dreaming to get it just right.

And as she watched her fellow agents disappear into the agency building, Agent Shadow glanced back over both shoulders to be sure there was no one from the Corn Pop Organization spying on them even now. An agent could never be too careful.

Two

"All right, highs and lows," Daddy said that night at the dinner table.

Sophie stuck her hand in the air before her older sister, Lacie, could start. At thirteen, Lacie could talk longer with her "lows" than their five-year-old brother, Zeke, could when he said the blessing.

"You don't have to raise your hand, Soph," Lacie said. "You're not in school."

"It's even Saturday," Zeke said. "You don't gotta do school stuff on Saturday."

Mama touched Zeke lightly on his just-like-Daddy's ski slope of a nose. "You don't HAVE to."

"That's what I said," Zeke said. Zeke's dark brown eyes—also like Daddy's—blinked. Except for his cut-with-a-weed-eater dark hair, he looked like Daddy in every way. So did Lacie for that matter. Only Sophie looked like Mama—all but Mama's highlighted hair.

"So what's your high, Soph?" Daddy said. He had invented the high/low thing at the dinner table so everybody could tell the best thing and the worst thing that happened to them that day.

"I want to tell my low first," Sophie said. "They're having a sixth-grade graduation dance for our end-of-the-year treat."

"Why is that a low, Sophie?" Mama said.

"Because it doesn't sound like that much fun—only it's also my high."

"You're going to have to explain that one," Daddy said.

"We could be here for days," Lacie muttered into her sloppy joe.

"We all decided—you know, Fiona and Maggie and Kitty and Darbie."

"The usual suspects." The laugh lines around Daddy's eyes crunched together.

"We all decided to get really dressed up."

"I love that!" Mama said. "Just do the girl thing—THAT sounds like fun."

Mama was chattering faster than Kitty, and Sophie had a feeling it was to keep Daddy from making some Dad-comment, like, "Your high is a dress?" He had come a long way since he and Mama and Sophie had been working with Dr. Peter, the Christian therapist, but sometimes he still didn't have a clue as far as Sophie was concerned.

Lacie dragged her napkin across her mouth, smearing a frown onto it. "I don't mean to take away from Sophie's high, but I'm going to need a new dress for my party too."

Daddy looked at Mama. "How much is this going to cost?"

"Not as much as you think. I'm going to make both of them, girls."

"Mo-om!" Lacie said.

But Sophie leaned forward, dipping the front of her tank top into the pool of ketchup next to her fries. "Do we get to pick out our own fabric?"

"And the pattern," Mama said. "Don't worry, Lacie, I won't make it look like I made it."

"No offense, Mom, but—"

"Wait," Daddy said. He looked at Lacie, eyes twinkling. "Is this your low?"

"It is now!"

While Lacie wailed about how the dress she really wanted was at Rave, and that since they had made the whole family change churches and took her away from all her friends at the old one, the least they could do was get her the *dress* she wanted—

Agent Shadow stood before the piles of fabric, rich with colors and textures—purple velvets, red silks, blue rhinestones that sparkled in the light. She had to remind herself, as she draped a filmy length of pink chiffon around her shoulders, that this was all in the line of duty.

"I personally washed that, so it isn't dirty," Lacie said. She snatched away the spoon Sophie was gazing into. "What are you looking at?"

The next day at Sunday school, while Fiona and Sophie were waiting for Darbie to come, Fiona said, "I'm supposed to go shopping with Miss Odetta Clide today." She rolled her eyes. "She is SO the worst nanny we've had yet."

"You're getting your dress for the dance already?" Sophie said. "That's cool!"

"I don't think so," Fiona said. "She'll make me get a dress from the Dark Ages—or worse."

"Is she still being super strict?" Sophie said.

"Strict? She's a prison guard! She actually made me go back and brush my teeth again this morning because she could still smell sausage on my breath." Fiona edged closer to Sophie and huffed out some air. "Can you smell it?"

"No."

"Boppa says she's giving us more structure and that we need that." Fiona sighed, the wayward piece of hair flopping across her eye. "Who would have thought my own grandfather would succumb to her?"

Sophie wanted to ask her what "succumb" meant, but Darbie had just walked in, and Sophie waved her over.

"Did you talk to your aunt about your dress?" Fiona said, instead of hello.

Darbie sniffed. "Did you have sausage for breakfast?" Then she grinned, showing the crooked teeth Sophie thought were kind of charming. "Aunt Emily nearly went off her nut, she was so excited. You'd think I was going to be married."

"NO," Fiona said. "Remember—no boys."

"No need to be reminding me." Darbie linked pinkies with both of them.

Between Sunday school and church, as the three of them dodged the crowd in the hallway to meet Sophie's family in the sanctuary, a familiar figure was suddenly beside them, barely taller than most of the sixth graders, except for Sophie, of course. Dr. Peter's eyes sparkled down at her through his glasses. His hair was Sunday-morning gelled, but the curls were popping out anyway. To Sophie, he was the best part about going to the new church.

"How are the Corn Flakes this morning?" he said.

"We're astonishingly good, Dr. P," Fiona said. Ever since she'd started going to church with Sophie back in March, Sophie had noticed that Fiona had tried every Sunday to use a new word for him. He usually seemed impressed.

"Good one, Fiona," he said. "And how's this wee lass?"

Darbie grinned again. Sophie knew she had taken to him right away, which was good, since she was going to see him

21

every week to help her deal with things like her mom and dad's deaths. Sophie used to see Dr. Peter every week too. Now she only went once a month for a "check-in," and she missed their weekly chats on his window seat.

"Still only three Flakes?" Dr. Peter said.

"Yes," Fiona said cheerfully. "Maggie and her mom go to a different church. And Kitty's parents don't even believe in church."

"And what are you going to do about it?" Dr. Peter said.

"Keep praying for Kitty," they all said together.

Sophie felt a little twinge somewhere. *I haven't exactly been praying that much lately*, she thought. She shut her eyes and tried to get Jesus into view.

Hello, she thought to him. *Um, I'm sorry—it's not that I don't love you. I just haven't had anything to ask you in a while.*

Yikes. What if God made something bad happen so she would pay more attention? Did it work that way? Was she going to be snatched from—from what?

From her post at the Secret Agency? Agent Shadow straightened her slim shoulders. NO, that couldn't happen. She would have to double her efforts to stay in contact with Headquarters. The Big Headquarters. In the sky. Especially with some unknown mission looming on the horizon.

"Sophie-Lophie-Loodle?"

Sophie shuddered back to Dr. Peter, who was peering at her as if he knew exactly where she'd been. He always used his nickname for her when he was calling her back.

"Did I miss something?" she said.

"Dr. Peter's Bible study starts Tuesday after school," Fiona said. "I can come if Miss Odetta Clide thinks I've gotten my room organized enough. Isn't there some kind of child labor law about that?"

"Maybe you can ask your parents about that," Dr. Peter said.

"Like I ever see them," Fiona said.

Sophie always felt bad for Fiona about how too busy her mom and dad always were—but right now she was smiling inside. She had been waiting for what seemed like a whole millennium for Dr. Peter to start the Bible study group. He was the one who had taught her how to read Bible stories, and doing that had helped her solve some *formidable* problems. That was another Fiona word.

"It's going to be just class!" That was a Darbie word—and it meant "very cool," only it sounded much more mature than plain cool.

That night when Sophie wiggled herself under her fluffy purple bedspread, she immediately closed her eyes and imagined Jesus, just the way Dr. Peter had taught her. She could almost see Jesus' kind eyes and his strong hands and she could ask him any question. The answers usually came later.

I'm really going to try to talk to you more, Sophie prayed when she got him in her mind. *Even if I don't actually have a question, which isn't so often because every time I think I have everything figured out—I SO don't! But I'm here, and if there's anything you want me to learn right now, please show me.*

She sighed as her thoughts grew fuzzy around the edges. *I don't guess you would want to hear about the perfect dress, would you? Gold satin with diamonds around the neck. Not real diamonds, of course.*

When Sophie met the Corn Flakes at their usual spot on the corner of the playground the next morning, Kitty started whining before Sophie could even get her backpack off.

"She's at it again," Darbie said. She and Fiona exchanged Kitty's-getting-on-my-nerves looks.

"What's wrong?" Sophie said.

"Her mom is making her wear one of her sisters' hand-me-down dresses to the dance," Maggie said.

"All those dresses are lame!" Kitty said. Her voice was getting up into only-dogs-can-hear territory. "All stupid ruffles and big old bows."

"That could be your cover though," Sophie said. "Who would think you were a secret agent dressed in some fluffy yellow thing?"

"I'll look like a canary!"

"Of course," Sophie said. "That's your new mission name. Canary."

"What's mine?" Maggie said. She was never the best at thinking up names.

"All three of you could have bird code names," Fiona said.

"I'm Heron," Darbie said. "Long legs and all that."

"I like Flamingo better," Sophie said.

"I'm not gonna be a buzzard," Maggie said with a voice-thud.

"No way," Fiona said. "You're more like an owl."

Maggie blinked.

"See what I mean?" Fiona said.

"Can I be Canary Louisa or something pretty like that?" Kitty said.

"That's too much for us to be saying to each other." Fiona said.

"But you can call yourself that," Sophie said quickly. She'd already heard enough whining and the bell hadn't even rung yet.

"What are you up to, Maggie?" Darbie said.

Sophie looked at Maggie, who was cocking her head with one eye closed, her lips bunched up into a pointy knot.

"I'm seeing what it feels like to be an owl," Maggie said.

Sophie giggled. Maggie hardly ever did the pretending thing unless somebody else did it first. *She's a Corn Flake to the core now*, she thought.

"You'll never get off the ground, Owl," Darbie said.

"WHOOO!" Maggie hooted.

She stretched her arms out and pulled her head down into her shoulders and made three leaps. Kitty squealed and clapped her hands.

"Again, again!" Darbie called out to Maggie.

Maggie looked back at them over her shoulder, still flapping her wings, and gave a wise wink. Fiona collapsed against Sophie, and they pounded on each other between guffaws.

"Go on then!" Darbie cried. "Fly!"

Maggie let out one more resounding "WHOOOO!" and thundered toward the middle of the playground, arms going so hard Sophie thought for a second she might take flight.

"It's a bird!" a male voice shouted.

"It's a plane!" another one yelled.

"It's SUPER BLIMP!" was the final cry.

On the other side of Maggie, the three Fruit Loops — Tod, Eddie, and Colton — fell into a heap, all puffing out their cheeks and poking out their stomachs.

Sophie watched as Maggie deflated like a leftover party balloon.

Three

The Corn Flakes had Maggie surrounded before the Fruit Loops could even pick their ridiculous selves up off the ground.

Darbie hollered at Eddie, "Are you talking about yourself, Whale Boy?"

"You know you're not a blimp, Mags," Fiona said as they practically carried Maggie back to their corner. "Not even close."

"You're NOT fat, Mags," Kitty sobbed. "You're not!"

"I know."

They all stopped in mid-hug to stare at Maggie. She just blinked, owl-like.

"They're only stupid boys," she said. "I don't pay any attention to what they say."

Darbie gave her an admiring nod. "You're a class person, Maggie LaQuita, and don't you be forgetting that." She ran a steely gaze over Fiona, Sophie, and Kitty. "We'd all do good to listen to her. Boys are a sorry lot."

"Blackguards," Fiona said. "They just proved it. Pinky promise — one more time."

There was pinky-linking all around before the bell rang.

"Maggie took that well, don't you think?" Sophie whispered to Fiona as they hurried off to language arts.

"She's resilient," Fiona said. "Fruit Loop slime slides right off her. That's why she's a great agent. Now, what we have to figure out, like, IMMEDIATELY, is how I'm going to get out of shopping with that evil Odetta Clide person. Did you know that she showed me pictures of herself going to her first dance — like a hundred years ago or something?" Fiona's gray eyes grew. "The Corn Pops are going to have a BLAST if I come in looking like that."

"We'll try to think of something," Sophie said.

They pinkied up.

"I want to say my high," Mama said at supper that night. She pushed Zeke's plate with the broccoli left on it toward him. "Here's your low, Z-Boy. Work on that while I'm talking."

Zeke pretended to throw up over the side of the chair. Mama's brown eyes got all bubbly as she ignored him and said, "I was on the phone all afternoon."

"That's your high?" Daddy said. "I thought you did that every day."

Mama spread out her fingers and counted on them. "I talked to Darbie's aunt, Maggie's mom, and Fiona's new nanny. What a lovely name: Odetta Clide."

Lacie choked over her iced tea glass. "Is this person actually living in the twenty-first century?"

"She is, and she's quite — something."

I bet, Sophie thought. *Something from the Dark Ages.*

"Where does the high come in?" Lacie said.

"The four of us are taking you two, Maggie, Fiona, and Darbie to Smithfield to have lunch and shop for party dresses."

Lacie dropped her fork into her pork chop. "You're going to BUY our dresses! Mama, you ROCK! Only—I think we should go to the mall in Virginia Beach. No offense, but what do they have in Smithfield?"

"Loveliness," Mama said. "It's old, and Darbie's aunt says there's a museum and all kinds of little shops and cafés. And no, I'm not going to buy your dresses. We're going there to get ideas."

"Oh." Lacie folded her arms. "You know, I bet I could just take the money you were going to use for fabric and buy something. They're having a sale at Rave."

Daddy shook his head. "Rave sells nothing but Band-Aids and dental floss. Off-limits, Lacie."

Mama got up to clear the table and Lacie followed, going off about how they treated her like a total baby. Sophie picked up her own plate, walked over to get Zeke's, and imagined herself shopping for her new disguise.

The lovely Smithfield boutique, where rack upon rack of elegant gowns awaited her choice. "It can't be anything showy," Agent Shadow told herself. She had to blend in. It was Canary and Flamingo and Owl who needed to stand out so they wouldn't LOOK like undercover agents. Canary in fluffy yellow acquired from her older sisters. Flamingo in hot pink. Owl in brown velvet that swayed as she danced with Edward Wornum, a.k.a. Whale Boy, who would whisper, eyes downcast, that he was sorry he had ever humiliated her by comparing her to a large, lighter-than-air craft—

"Quit blowing in my ear, Soph! That tickles!"

Zeke peeled his sticky palm from Sophie's, leaving her the last mouthful of broccoli he had spit into it.

"Already at the dance, Soph?" Daddy said. He grinned at her as he twirled her around, nearly knocking Lacie inside the dishwasher. "Just keep the daydreams here, huh? You don't want to lose your camera at this late date."

He was talking about the deal they had: if she made at least a B in everything, she got to keep her video camera, which meant limiting her dreaming to filming and keeping it out of the classroom, where she was supposed to pay attention.

"So can I call Fiona?" Sophie said to Mama as she washed the green off her hand. "Does she know about Saturday yet?"

Daddy leaned against the counter, elbows propped. "You're really into this dance thing, huh? I don't know why you want to complicate your life with boys."

"Eew!" Sophie said.

"Well, I assume there are going to be boys at this dance."

"I'm not going for the boys! Sick!"

"Good attitude, Soph," Daddy said. He put out his arm just as Lacie tried to make an exit from the kitchen and he hooked her in by the neck. "Now, you, on the other hand—"

Lacie started screeching again. Sophie loaded the silverware into the dishwasher, thoughts—and stomach—turning. *I don't even want to get anywhere CLOSE to a boy! Gross me out, why don't you?*

She tried to imagine sharp-faced Tod Ravelli, Mr. I'm So Cool I Can Hardly Stand It, holding out his hand to her, asking her to dance—but even Agent Shadow wouldn't go there. *"I won't even do it to capture spies from the Corn Pop Organization,"* the agent told herself. *"I have made a promise to my people that I will never break."*

It was obvious the next day that the Corn Pops had made no such promise to each another. During first period, Sophie saw Anne-Stuart go to the sharpener with a point already on her pencil, just because Tod was there. Second period, Ms. Quelling had to call on B.J. twice because she was so busy staring at Eddie.

How TOTALLY gross is that? Sophie thought.

The only thing grosser was Julia walking her fingers up Colton Messik's neck while they were standing in the lunch line. He reached back to grab her hand to make her stop, and then he twisted her arm around until she was almost on the floor.

She laughed up into his face like he was James Bond.

More like Pond, Sophie thought. *Pond SCUM.*

"I'd break his arm if he did that to me," said the girl behind Sophie.

It was Gill, one of the four athletic girls in their class who were friendly to the Corn Flakes. Sophie and Fiona had named Gill and her friends the Wheaties. Gill was lanky, with reddish hair and very green eyes.

"I think Julia likes it," Sophie said, nodding toward Julia, who was now weaving among the tables with Colton on her heels threatening her with his juice box.

"You know it," Gill said. She nudged Sophie lightly on the arm with her fist. "But what's to like about somebody trying to squirt you with grape juice?"

"And they say YOU guys are weird," said another Wheatie, a husky girl named Harley whose cheeks came up and made her eyes almost disappear when she smiled. "They're the weird ones."

The Corn Pops got weirder after lunch, when all the fourth, fifth, and sixth graders were seated around the edges of the cafeteria on floor mats for an assembly. Julia led her group to sit against the wall, right behind the Corn Flakes.

"What's this about anyway?" Sophie heard B.J. say.

"We get to see somebody do gymnastics," someone answered her.

Sophie took a peek. It was Willoughby. She was finger-twirling a piece of her wavy milk-chocolate-colored hair—worn in a short cut that was shorter in back than in front. One sandal-clad foot was wiggling too. Sophie had heard Julia tell her to "quit fidgeting—you're so annoying" more than once.

"All of us can do gymnastics," Julia said, flipping her burnt-auburn ponytail. "What's the big deal?"

"It's a boy," Willoughby said.

"A boy?" Anne-Stuart said.

"Oh, brother," Fiona whispered to Sophie. "I bet you ten dollars Julia's already putting on lip gloss."

"A boy from our class," Willoughby said.

"Nuh-uh," B.J. said.

Out of the corner of her eye, Sophie could see B.J. get up on her knees to scan the sixth grade.

"It's not somebody from our class, *Willoughby*," B.J. said. She sounded like she had something in her mouth she wanted to spit out. "The only boys who could do gymnastics in our class are Tod and Eddie and Colton, and they're all sitting out here."

"Eddie doing gymnastics?" Kitty whispered across Maggie, who was beside Sophie. "He'd break the floor."

"They're not the only boys in our class," Willoughby said.

But just then Mrs. Olinghouse, their tall principal with the silvery hair and the blue eyes that could slice through somebody, stepped up to a microphone in the corner. The whole cafeteria went silent.

"We have a special treat today, boys and girls," she said. "Many of you know this young man, but you don't know that he competes all over the country as a gymnast. And today, he's going to do a demonstration for you."

31

"Life's desire," Sophie heard Julia say behind her. "Wake me up when it's over."

"I can do a cartwheel," Colton Messik yelled to Mrs. Olinghouse.

"If you can do one like this boy, Colton, I will give you a day off."

"Sweet!"

"And now, boys and girls, I give you—Jimmy Wythe!"

"Jimmy WYTHE?" the Corn Pops said in unison.

"That kid who hangs out with the computer guys?" Maggie said to Sophie.

It was the same kid, suddenly doing double backflips across the padded floor and landing on his feet. For the next twenty minutes he didn't stop—skinny Jimmy Wythe, who didn't look so scrawny in his shiny one-piece suit. He had muscles where Eddie Wornom had baby fat, total control where Colton Messik stumbled over his own feet, and speed that would have left little Tod Ravelli in the dirt.

Colton is definitely not going to get his day off, Sophie thought.

Sophie had never really noticed blond-haired Jimmy Wythe much before—except for the fact that he, like his friends, kept pretty much to their computers and didn't make disgusting noises with their armpits and burp "Jingle Bells" the way the Fruit Loops did. Even Kitty had said she thought he was "mysterious."

But there was no missing Jimmy now. *He moves like a deer*, Sophie thought. *A deer that does somersaults and walks on his hands.*

Whenever he finished a part of his routine, shy Jimmy Wythe faced the audience, throwing his arms up and rewarding them with a smile that flashed white against his very tan skin. The kids cheered and whistled loud and high.

As he made his final bow, Kitty leaned across Maggie again and said, "He's a babe!" Her cheeks were watermelon red.

But Kitty's excitement couldn't compare to B.J.'s and Anne-Stuart's. They were screaming so loud, Sophie turned around to make sure they weren't dying. Anne-Stuart's pale blue eyes were about to wash right out of her head, as far as Sophie could tell, and B.J. was climbing up onto wiry little Willoughby's shoulders, craning for a last glimpse of Jimmy as he left the cafeteria with a wave.

"I thought they said he was a geek," Fiona said to Sophie.

"Well, they're going mental over him now," Darbie said.

Sophie felt herself grinning. *This is ALMOST as good as if one of us did it*, she thought. *He showed those Pops they're not the only ones who can do awesome things.*

When Mrs. Olinghouse dismissed them to go to fifth period, Anne-Stuart and B.J. climbed over Darbie and Fiona and raced for the door. By the time the Corn Flakes reached it, one of them was on each side of Jimmy, tugging at his sweaty arms and saying things like, "You were so GOOD!" And "I never knew you could do that!"

"They never knew he existed," Fiona muttered.

"He WAS good though," Maggie said.

"Sorry, Maggot," said Colton, grinning at Maggie from one stick-out ear to the other.

"It's about TIME you were apologizing," Darbie said.

"Nah," Colton said. "I'm sorry she doesn't have a chance with Jungle Gym Jimmy. I heard he doesn't like fat—"

"Close your cake trap, Colton," Darbie said.

Colton froze for a mini-second, and then grinned at Darbie. "Cake trap. That's pretty good. Hey, Eddie—close your cake trap, dude! Close your cake trap!"

"We're so out of here," Sophie said. She hauled Darbie and Fiona toward the math room before they had a chance to close Colton's cake trap for him. Kitty and Maggie had already disappeared.

"Why are those boys bugging us again?" Kitty whined while Mrs. Utley was handing out worksheets. "I thought they learned their lesson during the science project."

"I don't know," Darbie said, "but I'm dying to make them pay."

"But that isn't the Corn Flakes way," Sophie said. She handed Darbie a sheet from the stack Mrs. Utley put on their table.

"Besides," Maggie said, "it doesn't bother me. They're just stupid boys."

Mrs. Utley paused before she moved on to the Wheaties. "And my advice to you ladies," she said, her many soft chins jiggling happily, "is that you wait until they get a whole lot smarter before you have much to do with them."

"We hear you," Fiona said.

Mrs. Utley smiled and took her chins to the next table. By then the Corn Pops were all standing at the pencil sharpener next to the door. When it opened and Jimmy Wythe appeared, back in his jeans and T-shirt, Anne-Stuart twirled to face him, but not before B.J. got to him, grabbed him by the wrist, and dragged him toward the Corn Pops' table.

"I think B.J. won that round," Fiona said.

"That's because she mugged him!" Sophie said.

"Anne-Stuart won't be giving up," Darbie said.

Kitty giggled. "You can't blame her. He IS cute."

The four of them turned on her. "No BOYS!" they all hissed.

"Ladies," Mrs. Utley said. She was looking at the Corn Pops, but the Flakes zipped their mouths and hunkered down over their papers.

Before five minutes had passed, Mrs. Utley moved Jimmy back to his usual "computer geek" table with curly-haired Nathan and skinny Vincent and the round-faced twins, leaving B.J. to pout her lower lip out and Anne-Stuart to go to work writing in her fake-curlicue form what Sophie knew had to be a note.

When the bell rang and everyone burst from the room for the break before science, Sophie saw Anne-Stuart tuck the folded paper into the pocket of Jimmy's T-shirt, giggle into his face, and run off to catch up with her fellow Pops.

"But we have more important things to do," Agent Shadow told herself as she moved with the crowd out into the hallway. *"If I had time—if I didn't have spies to watch—I would like to say to Secret Weapon Wythe, 'You're better than all of them.'"*

"Thanks," someone said. Sophie felt her eyes widen. Beside her stood Jimmy Wythe. He smiled a shy smile at her and backed away into the hallway crowd.

"Did I say something to him?" Sophie said.

Kitty sighed, eyes in two dreamy puddles. "I don't know what it was—but I think he liked it."

"But somebody ELSE didn't like it." Maggie jerked her head toward the water fountain.

Anne-Stuart and B.J. stood there, holding Julia's hair back while she drank, looking dead-on at Sophie.

"I think they're wishing it was YOUR head in that sink so they could drown you," Darbie said.

Sophie didn't answer. She knew Darbie was right.

Four

Sophie didn't wait for bedtime that night. She went straight to her room after school and started praying *then*.

Sitting in the middle of her purple comforter, Sophie tried to imagine Jesus. As soon as his kind eyes came into view in her mind, the prayer-thoughts began. *Things aren't going so good. The Fruit Loops are trying to humiliate Maggie. B.J. and Anne-Stuart hate me more than ever now because they think I'm trying to steal the boy they like. And I don't even LIKE boys! Well, except for you. You were a boy. But I bet you never told any girl that she was a blimp or that she'd never get a boyfriend.*

Sophie fell back against her pile of pillows and grabbed one to hug against her. *What I want to ask you is—what do I do? I don't want them making fun of Maggie anymore. Right now, I really wish I WAS a secret agent so I could just turn them in to the government ...*

Agent Shadow clicked the last pair of handcuffs on the third prisoner. Colton Messik was pale to the tips of his stick-out ears. He SHOULD be ashamed, the agent thought to herself. He tried to make the Owl feel bad about herself when she was in the line of duty, doing important work to do away with the likes of him and his Fruit Loop Mob. Agent Shadow breathed a deep sigh of relief

*as she shoved Colton Messik and his two accomplices toward the
armored car, which would take them straight to solitary confine-
ment in a maximum security prison. There wouldn't even be a
trial. Everyone knew they were guilty . . .*

Sophie opened her eyes and felt a smile cross her face.
Putting the Fruit Loops in their place—now THAT was a
mission worth going to a dance for.

By Saturday, the Loops and the Pops were miles from
Sophie's mind as everyone climbed into Fiona's family's big
Ford Expedition to head for Smithfield.

For the first twenty minutes of the trip, Sophie's attention was on Miss Odetta Clide, who was gripping the steering
wheel with the veins on her hands bulging like blue twine.
Her wiry gray hair was short and pushed back from her face
with the brush marks still in it. *That hair wouldn't DARE fall in
her eyes*, Sophie thought.

Miss Odetta kept glancing into the rearview mirror as if
she didn't want those eyes to miss a thing somebody might be
doing wrong. Before they had even gotten into the car while
in Fiona's driveway, she had made Fiona go back in and put a
barrette in her hair.

"She's just as strict as you said," Sophie whispered to Fiona
in the far backseat.

"You haven't seen anything yet," Fiona whispered back.
"But we can't talk about it now or she'll give me demerits for
whispering. She says it's rude."

"Fiona—that's five demerits," said Miss Odetta Clide. "A
lady does not whisper in the presence of others." Her eyes, a
washed-out blue, were watching them in the rearview mirror.

"What are demerits?" Maggie said.

"Marks for being rude, inconsiderate, or irresponsible,"
Miss Odetta Clide said.

Fiona slid down in the seat.

"Do you get in trouble for them?" Maggie said.

"If Fiona accumulates too many she will."

Fiona slid farther.

"How many is too many?" Maggie said.

"Margarita!" her mom said.

"Not as many as you might think," said Miss Odetta Clide. And once again she gave Fiona a look in the mirror—although by now Sophie was sure she could no longer see her. Fiona was almost on the floor.

But even that was forgotten the minute they arrived in Smithfield.

"This is a beautiful little town!" Mama said.

"Isn't it precious?" Darbie's aunt Emily said.

Sophie didn't think *precious* was exactly the right word for the old courthouse that stood on the street like a wise judge—and the country store with two bent men playing checkers out front—and the ice cream parlor where she was sure they still made ice cream the old-fashioned way, whatever that was.

"It's nostalgic," said Fiona. She emerged from hiding and pressed her face to the car window between Sophie's and Darbie's.

"Look at these gorgeous Victorian homes," Mama said. "It makes you want to wear a bustle, doesn't it?"

"You'll see houses from the Federal and Georgian periods as well," Miss Odetta Clide said as if she were reading from a textbook. "A few Colonial. This town is over 250 years old. It was the peanut capital of the world at one time." Miss Odetta parked the Expedition and turned stiffly to the backseat. "A lady listens, Fiona," she said. "She learns."

Fiona moaned—although not loud enough for Miss Odetta Clide to catch her. Sophie couldn't even imagine how many demerits that would be worth.

But after they parked and started down Main Street, past the bakery and the antique stores and the houses with their wide porches, Sophie found herself sidling closer to Miss Odetta to hear what she was saying.

"British merchants started settling here in about 1752," she said in her brisk-for-an-older-lady voice. "Brought in by the sea captains up the Pagan River."

"Look at those roses," Mama said.

They stopped to look up at a house with thick white columns on its porch.

"Now this one is Civil War era," Miss Odetta said. "Might have been owned by a steamboat captain. They brought their boats up the river too, after the war, trying to build things up again."

"Would their wives have waited for them on that porch?" Sophie said.

Miss Odetta Clide squinted down at her as if she'd just noticed Sophie was there. "It would be safe to say they might have. The reason they built the porches so deep was to accommodate the women's dresses. A hoopskirt could reach from the front door to the railing. And the women were even more extravagant in the Victorian period. You need only look at their homes."

She clipped around the corner with everyone right behind her. Miss Odetta stopped in front of a pale blue house that had towers and turrets like a castle, stained-glass windows, and trim that reminded Sophie of a fancy gingerbread house.

"This is Victorian," Miss Odetta said. "The ladies who first lived in this place wore the bustles Mrs. LaCroix spoke of, and corsets pulled so tight they could barely draw breath."

"Why would they want to do that?" Maggie said. "Sounds brutal."

"That is precisely what THEIR daughters said. In the 1920s they threw away the corsets and replaced them with short dresses that had everyone scandalized. No one had ever seen a woman's legs in public before."

"What's 'scandalized' mean?" Sophie whispered to Fiona.

"It's like shocked right out of their Sketchers," Fiona whispered back.

Miss Odetta turned from the Victorian mansion to gaze down at the Corn Flakes. Sophie tugged at her sundress to make it look longer.

"I understand we are looking at party dresses today."

"Mama and I are just getting ideas," Sophie said. "Ma'am." She wondered if Fiona's friends could get demerits slapped on them too.

"Smithfield is the place to do that. You will see every kind of garment from a Colonial ball gown to a Roaring Twenties flapper dress. The possibilities are endless."

They visited the Isle of Wight Museum, which was set up in a country store from the early 1900s. There were displays of cheese wheels and thread and shoes and cake boxes and washboards. They followed Miss Odetta to some sassy dresses that hung on the wall.

"The forerunners of the miniskirt," Miss Odetta said. "Vintage 1921."

Some had fringe, others sequins, and still others were draped with feather boas that must have left some poor ostrich naked. All of them were straight, falling from the shoulders to the knees in one long line. They didn't do much for Sophie's imagination.

But Darbie ran right up to them, arms outstretched—until Miss Odetta told her a lady didn't touch antiques. Still, Darbie stood there with her hands clenched behind her back, the sequins sparkling in her eyes.

"I ADORE these!" she said. "Aren't they just CLASS?"

"And just a little out of our price range, Darbie honey," Aunt Emily said.

Senora LaQuita put her hand on Aunt Emily's arm. "I can design this for Darbie," she said, trilling the "r" in the way Sophie loved.

Darbie looked at her aunt, biting her lower lip.

"I don't know what to say," Aunt Emily said. "That's such a nice offer."

"Say yes," Maggie said. "My mother wouldn't offer if she didn't mean it."

"Well—if that's what you want, Darbie."

"I do! These were MADE for me!"

"That's one, then," Miss Odetta said. "Shall we continue?"

From there it was decided by the Corn Flakes that they would each choose a dress from the time period that, as Fiona put it, "spoke to them." It was just what secret agents would do to conceal their identities from an enemy mob like the Fruit Loops, Sophie was sure.

As they twirled and giggled and squealed through the antique shops and the art galleries, Maggie decided she liked the dresses the Victorian girls wore. Fiona went for a Civil War look with ruffles and a full skirt. Miss Odetta Clide nixed a hoopskirt, but she agreed that they could use Fiona's dress money to have Maggie's mom design one for her.

When Sophie stood for five minutes in front of a painting of a Colonial family, gazing at the young girl in the gold dress with lace around the scoop neck and sleeves that flared out deliciously at the elbows, Mama whispered to her, "I'll see what I can do, Dream Girl."

When they got back to Poquoson, it was too hard to go their separate ways, and they wanted to share their news with Kitty so she wouldn't be left out. Their faces were long as they pulled into Fiona's driveway.

Boppa met them and told Miss Odetta Clide she might need to go inside and do some damage control, since he had been with Fiona's little brother and sister all day. When she was gone, Boppa said, "These girls are going to go into mourning if we don't let them have a sleepover tonight. What do you say, ladies? I'll make them go to bed early."

Mama smiled. "So you're afraid of her too, huh, Boppa?"

Within the hour, the Corn Flakes had returned with pajamas and sleeping bags and Kitty, and they were busily writing down script ideas when they heard a knock at Fiona's bedroom door. They were afraid it was Miss Odetta telling them to turn out the light. But it was Boppa, smiling his soft smile and wiggling his dark caterpillar eyebrows and running his hand over the top of his bald head.

"Anybody up for some dancing lessons?" he said.

"Dancing lessons, Boppa?" Fiona said as they all skittered after him down the hall to the door that led out to the deck.

"I hear you're going to a dance. You've got the dresses taken care of—now you need to learn how to dance."

Boppa had the picnic table scooted out of the way with a boom box on it, and there was a string of white lights twinkling in the May night.

"I know you kids THINK you know how to dance," he said.

"I don't," Maggie said.

"But I'm going to teach you some real dances. We're going to start with the bop."

"I like that word!" Kitty said, giggling. "I want to bop!"

"Come on then," Boppa said. He poked the play button and held out his hand to Kitty. She plunked hers right into it just as a man on the CD started singing about a hound dog.

"I know this song!" Kitty squealed. "My grandma taught me how to play it on the piano!"

"This is Elvis Presley, ladies," Boppa said. "The King of Rock 'n' Roll. Come on—grab a partner."

Before the song was over, Sophie and Fiona had the bop down, and Darbie and Maggie, while they were still slamming into each other at times, were getting close.

After that Boppa taught them to waltz and then cha-cha. The waltz was Sophie's favorite—she could imagine herself in the gold dress with the flared sleeves, sweeping across the floor—but she was doing more stumbling than sweeping.

"Help me, Boppa!" she said, after she stepped on Fiona's foot for the thirtieth time and Fiona refused to be her partner until her bruises healed.

"Miss Odetta Clide, do you waltz?"

They all looked up to see Miss Odetta in the doorway, arms folded. "Of course I waltz. Every well-trained lady knows how to waltz."

"Then please do me the honor of helping me with a demonstration."

Boppa held out his hand to Miss Odetta. Kitty giggled. Maggie blinked like an owl. Fiona slithered down onto the picnic table bench.

But when Miss Odetta Clide slid her hand into his and placed the other one on his arm and they began to move in a smooth one-two-three, one-two-three across the deck, all mouths fell open. "That is class," Darbie whispered.

Boppa and Miss Odetta were floating, looking directly into each other's eyes like they didn't even have to be aware of the feet that carried them in swooping circles across the ballroom floor.

Agent Shadow lifted her eyes from the skirt of her golden dress to the face of the Unknown Dancer and let him take her hand. Gracefully they swished past the awestruck crowd. "I must remember to keep my mind on the mission at hand," she told herself. But just then, she couldn't remember what it was.

Five

For Sophie, time spun in a waltz of its own after their dancing lesson.

On Sunday, Dr. Peter reminded the girls that their Bible study would start Tuesday. Sophie felt a twinge again — the kind she used to feel when she forgot a homework assignment.

I'm going to read my Bible and pray every night from now on, she thought.

But Sunday night there was homework, and Monday after school she went fabric shopping with Mama. When Sophie headed for the pattern books at Jo-Ann Fabrics & Crafts, Mama said, "We won't be needing those, Dream Girl. Senora LaQuita told me she would teach me how to design my own patterns." She gave Sophie a wispy Mama-smile. "It's time I learned anyway. Who knows, maybe I can whip up something like they sell at Rave for Lacie."

"Anybody can make Band-Aids, Mama," Sophie said.

They found gold taffeta and brown shimmering lace, and Sophie was so thrilled she barely noticed the Fruit Loops or the Corn Pops all day Tuesday.

What did get her attention was Kitty.

Kitty giggled a lot that morning, more than usual, and it was a different kind of giggling. She laughed when things weren't even funny—like when Gill lost a filling out of her tooth, right into the burrito Maggie gave her from her lunch. Kitty's voice was shrill, and the laughter didn't get to her eyes.

When they went out to the playground during the second half of lunch period to rehearse for their film, Fiona put her hands on her almost-hips and said, "All right, Kitty, you're hiding something. What is it?"

Kitty's eyes got as big as cereal bowls. "How did you know?"

It's a good thing Kitty doesn't try to be a REAL secret agent, Sophie thought.

"Because you've been acting mental all day," Darbie said.

Kitty sank down to the ground and leaned against the fence, knees pulled into her chest. "You're all going to be mad at me when I tell you—and you're probably gonna kick me out of the Corn Flakes—but I never wanted to agree to that pack thing anyway."

"What pack thing?" Maggie said.

Sophie nodded. "You mean the 'pact'? About the boys?"

"Yes," Kitty said. "I hate the Fruit Loops, but I like other boys—nice boys—and I found one. And you can't make me not go to the dance with him!"

She burst into the tears Sophie had been expecting. Maggie reached into her backpack and handed Kitty a tissue.

"You don't mean some boy asked you?" Darbie said.

"And you said yes?" Fiona said.

Kitty nodded as she blubbered into the wadded-up tissue.

"I'm scandalized," Fiona said.

Sophie sat down next to Kitty. "Who is he?" she said.

"Nathan Coffey," she said, although from the other side of the tissue it sounded at first like "make some toffee."

"Which one is he again?" Darbie said.

"Curly hair. Braces," Fiona said. "Wears a Redskins hat."

"Remember I told you his dad is in my dad's squadron," Kitty said. "We even went camping with them last summer." She looked up, face streaming and miserable. "I didn't know I had a crush on him before."

Maggie said, "How can you have a crush on somebody and not even know it?"

"All right, let's not all go off our nut here," Darbie said. She sat down and pulled Fiona with her. Maggie squatted beside them.

"You're not in love with Nathan, Kitty," Fiona said, her face serious and sage.

"We're going together," Kitty said. She poked her chin into the tops of her knees.

"Where are you going?" Maggie said.

"I think that means they're boyfriend and girlfriend," Sophie said.

"And THAT means you're breaking the Corn Flakes pact," Fiona said.

Darbie shook her head. "You're making a bags of it, Kitty, I'm telling ya."

Kitty looked at Sophie with panic in her eyes. "Are you going to throw me out?"

"No!" Sophie said, before Fiona could jump in with something Sophie knew she would have to apologize for seven hundred times later.

"If she goes, I go," Maggie said. She even stood up.

"She's not going!" Sophie said.

Kitty flung herself at Sophie's neck and cried until the bell rang, while Fiona and Darbie folded their arms and looked everywhere but at Kitty.

On their way to class, Fiona pulled Sophie back. "What is the point of having a pact if you can just break it and nothing happens?"

"I don't know," Sophie said. "But Dr. Peter will."

Fiona's eyebrows came together. "I thought he was going to talk about the Bible."

"Stuff like that is in the Bible," Sophie said.

There was another Jesus-twinge. *I'm coming back*, she prayed. *Honest, I am.*

It was so much easier to remember to talk to Jesus when Dr. Peter was around. And just as Sophie had expected, he had the Bible study room fixed up so that everybody said some form of "Wow!" when they walked in.

"Everybody" consisted of Sophie, Fiona, Darbie, and Harley and Gill from the Wheaties.

"I didn't know you went to church here, Harley!" Sophie said.

"We don't," Gill said. "Not yet anyway." She always talked for the husky Harley, who just smiled that eyes-disappearing-into-cheeks smile a lot. "Your mom told my mom about this at a PTO meeting, so she's making me try it."

"I don't want anyone to come because her mom makes her," Dr. Peter said. "But I am going to ask you to give it an honest try. Two sessions. Then if you would rather do something else with your time, I'll tell your moms they should let you." Dr. Peter clapped his hands together and nodded toward the beanbag chairs that were set in a circle, each one a different color. "Choose a seat, and let's get started."

Sophie picked the purple chair and flopped into it. Beside each beanbag was a Bible in a matching color.

"This is class," Darbie whispered to her.

"A lady doesn't whisper," Fiona said.

"I don't know about a lady," said Dr. Peter. "But members of this group don't HAVE to whisper—at least not in here."

"Define this group," Fiona said.

"We're going to do that over time," Dr. Peter said. "But I will tell you this: you wouldn't be here if you weren't ready to get closer to God." He wrinkled his nose so that his glasses worked their way back up closer to his sparkling eyes. "Unless your mom made you come."

"It's cool so far," Gill said. Harley gave him a thumbs-up.

"You all got the packet I sent you, telling you what we're going to be doing?"

Heads bobbed.

"So, any questions before we get started?"

"I have one," Fiona said. She resituated herself in her hot pink beanbag. "Sophie says the Bible talks about stuff like what we're dealing with right now with a friend of ours. I just don't see how that could be true, since the Bible was written, like, a million years ago."

Sophie was sure Miss Odetta Clide would say a lady didn't talk to the Bible study teacher like that. But Dr. Peter grinned at Fiona.

"I like a challenge," he said. "Bring it on."

Fiona straightened up tall, and then looked at Gill and Harley. "You guys have to promise you won't tell anybody at school about this."

"What is said in here stays in here," Dr. Peter said. "That's one of the ground rules. But we aren't here to vent about people either."

"This isn't venting. Here's what happened."

Fiona told him all about the pact and Kitty's breaking it, with Darbie and Sophie adding details, and Harley and

Gill looking as if they were hearing about the worst kind of traitor.

"So," Fiona said when they were through, "how can the Bible tell us what to do about something that probably never happened back then?"

"The Bible is full of stories about betrayal," Dr. Peter said. He rubbed his hands together as if he couldn't wait to get into one.

"Oh," Fiona said. "So what's the answer?"

"What's the question?" Dr. Peter said. He looked at the Wheaties. "Do you two mind if we explore that?"

Gill was obviously into the whole thing, which meant Harley was too.

"The question is—" Fiona looked at Darbie.

"Why would an eleven-year-old girl be wanting a boy-friend?" Darbie said.

"So much that she would break the pact," Sophie put in. "We made a promise to each other that we wouldn't go to the dance with a boy—any of us."

"Did Kitty agree to the promise?" Dr. Peter said.

"Yes!" Fiona said. "She pinkied up like the rest of us."

Dr. Peter looked bewildered. Sophie and Darbie linked pinky fingers, and he nodded. "Gotcha," he said.

"But then today she's telling us she never wanted to make the promise in the beginning," Darbie said.

Dr. Peter ran his finger up and down his nose. "Something is really strong in her to make her break a promise. Maybe the Bible can show us what that something is."

"No way," Gill said.

"That's what I'm thinking," Fiona said.

"Don't take my word for it," Dr. Peter said. "Let's go in."

Sophie was squirming in the purple beanbag, but Dr. Peter's eyes were still dancing, the way they did when there was a juicy problem to solve.

"Turn to Ecclesiastes 3 — that's in the Old Testament, Fiona. There you go." Dr. Peter glanced around the circle as they thumbed to the right place. "This isn't the most uplifting book in the Bible, but I think you'll like this part. Now, I want you to close your eyes and imagine that you have come to a wise teacher, someone you look up to."

Sophie chose Dr. Peter and pictured him in her mind with a beard down to his chest and wearing a long robe that touched the tops of his rope sandals.

"Imagine you have come to this teacher with your question about Kitty, and you know he or she will give you the right answer."

"What's the question again?" Gill said.

"What is so strong in Kitty that she would break her pact with her friends? What does she think is so important that she would do this? Now picture yourself asking this wise person that question. Hear it coming out of your mouth. Be aware of how you're sitting and what you're feeling. Be there."

Sophie was already there, sitting at Dr. Peter's feet, looking up at him with begging eyes, wanting so much to know the answer before they lost Kitty to some boy who would never be as nice and loyal to her as the Corn Flakes were. She could even feel the knot in her throat.

"Now," Dr. Peter said, "I want you to hear these words as if they are coming from the teacher's mouth — the answer to your question."

"'There is a time for everything,'" he read, "'and a season for every activity under heaven: a time to be born and a time to die, a time to plant and a time to uproot, a time to kill and a time to heal, a time to tear down and a time to build.' "

He went on to read about weeping and laughing, mourning and dancing, scattering and gathering, hugging and not hugging. Sophie listened, waiting for the part where she would have the oh-I-get-it feeling. So far what he was reading was only making the knot in her throat bigger, and she didn't know why.

" 'A time to search and a time to give up' " Dr. Peter read, " 'a time to keep and a time to throw away, a time to tear and a time to mend.' "

She heard an impatient sigh from Fiona.

" 'A time to be silent and a time to speak, a time to love and a time to hate, a time for war and a time for peace.' "

It was quiet, except for the sound of someone trying not to cry out loud.

"You okay, Loodle?" Dr. Peter said.

"No," Sophie said. She smeared her arm across her wet eyes. "Everything is changing. It doesn't ever stay the same. Next year we'll be in middle school, and all the Corn Flakes might not be together. And it might be harder, and I might start doing bad again and get the camera taken away. And maybe Kitty really will decide a boy is better than us, and she'll go away because it's her time to do that."

"That's what those verses mean, isn't it?" Darbie said. "That there's a time for every different thing."

"When is my time to kill?" Fiona said brightly. "There are a few Fruit Loops I'd like to take out."

Dr. Peter grinned. "I doubt that time is now, so hold off."

Harley and Gill looked disappointed.

"Sometimes change is hard," Dr. Peter said, looking at Sophie. "Especially when you like things the way they are right now. It's okay to feel bad over that for a while, as long as you know another time will come with its own set of good things."

"So let me get this straight," Fiona said. "It's Kitty's time to start liking boys."

"That could be part of it," Dr. Peter said.

"I'm not in that time yet," Fiona said.

"Me either," Sophie said.

Harley and Gill were shaking their heads. "I'm not ever having that time," Gill said. "No way."

Dr. Peter cocked his head at Darbie. "You want to tell us what you're thinking?"

"I'm thinking it seems to me it's a bit early for Kitty to be having this time," Darbie answered.

"I definitely don't like this pairing-up thing in the sixth grade," Dr. Peter said. "But there's nothing wrong with discovering that there is more to boys than nose-picking and smelly socks."

"That's so FOUL!" Fiona said.

Darbie was studying Dr. Peter's face like she was following a map.

"So how do we know when it's OUR time?" she said. "When it's okay to really like a boy and maybe want to dance with him or something."

Fiona looked at Darbie in horror.

"That's a great question," Dr. Peter said. "You'll know it's your time for boys when being around them takes you closer to God, not farther away." He rubbed his hands together. "And getting closer to God is what we're going to learn how to do, using the Bible as our guide."

I wish Kitty were here, Sophie thought as she flipped through the Bible to the next verses Dr. Peter called out. *I'm not sure she's close to God at all.*

Kitty always bowed her head and closed her eyes when the Corn Flakes prayed together, but Sophie wasn't sure it was always God she was thinking about.

Right now, she was pretty sure it was nobody but Nathan Coffey.

Six

Over the next few days, Sophie was more and more sure she was right about Kitty's concentrating on Nathan and not God. When the Corn Flakes met before school and between classes and during lunch, and even when they got together outside of school to rehearse for filming their movie—*Secret Agents at the Ball*—all Kitty could talk about was her "boyfriend."

"If he's your boyfriend," Fiona said to Kitty on Thursday in the hall, "why aren't you ever with him?"

"I'm with him!" Kitty said. Sophie wasn't surprised to hear Kitty's voice winding up as she continued. "We talk on the phone every night, and he writes me notes, and this Sunday my family and his family are going to the beach."

"But that's not really a date," Maggie said.

"So?" Kitty folded her arms up under her green poncho. "We're still going to be together."

"Just don't be holding hands or any of that," Darbie said.

Kitty turned a guilty red, like she'd already been considering it. The very thought made Sophie's own palms go sweaty. *Ew,* she thought.

But at least Kitty's liking Nathan wasn't as bad as Anne-Stuart and B.J. going after Jimmy Wythe. The day of the spelling bee in Mr. Denton's class, B.J. actually shoved Anne-Stuart into a bookcase so she could stand next to Jimmy.

Sophie tried not to grin too big at Fiona when B.J. missed the first word Mr. Denton gave her, which obviously happened because B.J. was so busy playing with the belt loops on Jimmy's khakis that she didn't even think about it.

"Opportunity without the *t*," Fiona whispered to Sophie. "How could she make a lame mistake like that?"

When B.J. had to sit down, Anne-Stuart wasted no time in getting as close to Jimmy as she could, whispering who-knew-what into his ear, while on the other side of Jimmy, Ross and Ian — the moon-faced twins — both looked like they were going to explode if they weren't allowed to laugh soon. Jimmy's cheeks practically turned purple, Sophie noted. *Mine would too if Anne-Stuart was that close to ME with her drippy nose*, she thought. Sophie didn't blame him for misspelling *his* next word so he could get away from her.

I think "B.J." stands for "Boy Jumper," Sophie thought. As soon as the bell rang, B.J. was on Jimmy's trail, unzipping his backpack and sticking a note inside.

Even if I liked Jimmy as much as she does, Sophie told herself, *WHICH I DON'T — I wouldn't be all in his space all the time.*

In Ms. Quelling's class, when Jimmy said hi to Sophie on the way to his table, she ducked behind *Traditional Spanish Food* — after she smiled back.

It was Friday morning before Sophie noticed that Darbie was being unusually quiet. When Maggie had to tell her twice that the bell had just rung and she needed to get to class, Darbie said that she hadn't heard it. But when Darbie didn't go to the restroom with the Corn Flakes between first and second periods—which she *always* did—Sophie got the feeling that she was keeping something from them.

"Does anybody know what's wrong with Darbie?" she said from her stall.

"Is something wrong with Darbie?" Kitty said from the next one.

Fiona was at the sink washing her hands. "How would you notice, Kitty? All you do is look at Nathan all the time."

Kitty's giggle bounced off the tile walls. "He's cute!"

"Yeah, we know," Fiona said. "You have it written all over your notebooks."

"Does she really, Maggie?" Sophie said.

"Maggie's not here," Fiona said. "She already left."

"Without US?" Kitty said.

Come to think of it, Sophie mused, *Maggie has been acting funny too. But not nervous-strange like Darbie. More like sad-strange.*

As they headed for the social studies room, Sophie wondered if Maggie was strange because Darbie and Sophie and Fiona were all going to Bible study and she wasn't. Sophie slipped into their table just as the bell rang and leaned over to Maggie in the chair next to her.

"Do you want to start going to Bible study with us on Tuesdays?" she said. "It's way cool. I bet your mom would let you."

Maggie looked up from the back of the notebook she was doodling on and gave Sophie a droopy-eyed smile. "I'll ask," she said.

Sophie was pretty sure Maggie wasn't cheered up.

At lunch Sophie wolfed down her peanut butter and pickle sandwich and watched Maggie push her red beans and rice around in their container and then pass it on to Harley.

"Those guys are watching us," Kitty said.

"What guys?" Fiona said.

Kitty pointed to a table on the other side of the Corn Pops, where Jimmy, Nathan, and Vincent immediately lowered their heads and examined their milk cartons.

"Check out the Corn Pops," Fiona said. "They thought Jimmy was looking at them."

Anne-Stuart and B.J. were giggling and going blotchy red. Even Julia rolled her eyes at the boys' table, although she quickly returned her attention to Colton, who was sitting next to her, tying her ponytail in a knot.

"If anybody else did that, she'd deck them," Fiona said. "Right, Darbie?"

"Huh?" Darbie said.

"I knew you weren't paying attention." Fiona drummed her fingers on the tabletop. "All right—what's up with you? Come on, you have to tell us. We're your best friends."

"Sophie, I believe we have a date."

Sophie jumped, nearly knocking Ms. Quelling's soda can out of her hand. Sophie had forgotten she had lunch detention for daydreaming in class that day.

"Yes, ma'am," Sophie said.

She got up and whispered to Fiona behind her backpack, "Find out what's wrong with Darbie."

Although Sophie had to sit in Ms. Quelling's classroom for only fifteen minutes, it felt like seven hours before the bell rang and she darted out into the hall to meet Fiona and Kitty.

"What did you find out?" Sophie said.

"Nothing!" Kitty, of course, whined.

"She said we'd be mad at her if she told us," Fiona said. "I said we'd be madder if she DIDN'T tell us, but she still wouldn't spill it." She nudged Sophie with her elbow. "I bet she would have if you'd been there."

"Go talk to her, Soph," Kitty said.

"Where is she?" Sophie said, heading farther up the hall-way at a faster pace.

"Look in the arts room—she SO didn't want to be around us," Fiona said. "She's acting like Kitty before she told us about Nathan—"

"Not Darbie!" Sophie called over her shoulder. "She's the one that came up with the pact in the first place!"

"I know what's wrong with Darbie."

Sophie turned around. Corn Pop Willoughby stood there, talking out of a small hole she made in the side of her mouth.

"I heard y'all talking," Willoughby said. "I know why Darbie thinks you'll be mad at her."

Sophie's thoughts flipped back and forth. *Listen to her, because you need all the information you can get. Don't listen to her, because she's a Corn Pop. Listen to her. Don't listen to her.*

Willoughby grabbed Sophie's wrist and pulled her toward the wall. The rest of the sixth graders surged past them. "Ross told me that Ian said that Darbie told him not to tell anybody because all her friends would be mad at her."

Sophie shook her head while she tried to sort that out. "Tell what?" she said.

"That she's going to the dance with Ian."

"Nuh-uh!"

"Yuh-huh. I know because I'm going with Ross, and he knows because Ian is his twin brother. Well, you knew that."

Sophie stared at Willoughby, whose very round hazel eyes quickly surveyed the crowd behind them. She drew in closer.

"Don't tell Julia and them that I'm going with Ross, okay? They think he's a geek, and they'll be telling me that every minute." She tightened her mouth hole. "I don't think I care what they think anymore, but I can't tell them that. You know how mean they can be."

But the Corn Pops were the farthest thing from Sophie's mind.

Finding Darbie — that was the only thing she could think about.

Seven

Sophie rounded a corner and saw Darbie coming out of the girls' restroom. When Darbie dived back in, Sophie dived in after her.

"When did he ask you?" Sophie said.

Darbie scowled at Sophie in the mirror. "Who's the blaggard who told you?"

"That's not what matters!"

"Yesterday," Darbie said. "And don't be asking me why I said yes because I don't know. He took me by surprise—I never thought any boy would ever be looking at me."

"I didn't think you WANTED them to look!"

"I didn't! Until yesterday when he asked me." Darbie's face softened as she turned to face Sophie. "It's different just talking about it, and actually having it happen. I don't know, Sophie. It just made me feel special."

"A BOY made you feel special?"

Darbie nibbled at her thumbnail. "It's different for me. Nothing special ever happened to me growing up in Ireland. It was all about keeping from getting hit in the head with a brick."

"Do you think it's your time to like boys?" Sophie said.

"Maybe it is." Darbie was almost whispering. "But I'm not thinking more about Ian than I am about God. I even thanked God last night for Ian's asking me. But I still want to be a Corn Flake." Her face scrunched up into a knot. "You let Kitty!"

Sophie didn't even hesitate. She put her arms around Darbie's neck. "We'll let you too," she said.

Darbie—who wasn't the hugging kind—clung to Sophie and whispered, "It's nice to have a boy liking you, Sophie. Just wait till it happens to you."

But Sophie was sure that was one thing she was never going to experience.

The next morning, Sophie and Fiona talked alone together as they walked to meet the other Corn Flakes on the playground.

"It isn't our time," Sophie said. "That's all there is to it."

"It's our time to be best friends forever," Fiona said. "I don't see how any boy could be as amazing to hang out with as you are."

"That's how I feel about you!" Sophie said just as they joined Darbie, Kitty, and Maggie at the fence. Sophie continued. "Could you even imagine one of the Fruit Loops doing a film with us?"

"Sure," Fiona said. "It would be a horror film."

Darbie and Kitty started giggling.

"They would make fantastic monsters," Sophie said. "We wouldn't even have to give them masks!"

"All they would have to do is be themselves." Fiona shuddered. "It would be so heinous nobody would watch it."

Darbie and Kitty collapsed against the fence.

But Maggie didn't seem to be enjoying the moment. She dug into her backpack and produced one of Senora LaQuita's breakfast burritos wrapped in paper.

"Anybody want this?" she said.

"I'll have a taste," Darbie said.

"How come you're not eating it, Maggie?" Fiona eyed her suspiciously. "You hardly eat anything anymore."

Maggie shrugged. "Not hungry."

Maggie looked as if she were about to pull imaginary covers over her head.

"Are you coming to Bible study with us tomorrow, Maggie?" Sophie said quickly.

"I wish I could go!" Kitty wailed. "My dad won't let me though. He says the next thing you know, somebody from the church will be at our door asking for money."

"*What?*" Fiona said to her.

But Sophie stayed focused on Maggie. "Will you come?" she said.

"Yeah," Maggie said. "My mother said I could."

"That is so cool!" Sophie knew her voice was squeaking, but somehow she had to make up for the way Maggie's was thudding. "And Saturday we have fittings at your house."

"Yay!" Kitty said. "Party dresses!"

"I thought you were wearing one of your sisters' hand-me-downs," Darbie said.

Kitty wrinkled her little china nose. "I am — but Maggie's mom said she would — what's that word, Mags?"

"Alter it."

"Yeah — she said she'd fix it any way I wanted! I'm gonna ask her to make it shorter."

"Then we have LOTS to look forward to," Sophie said. She nodded at Maggie until Maggie gave her a grudging nod back.

"What's going on over there?" Darbie said.

Sophie swiveled around in time to see B.J. picking herself up from the ground and wiping off the seat of her red Capris with slapping hands. Her cheeks matched the color of her pants as she bore down on Anne-Stuart like a cornered Siamese cat.

"Uh-oh," Fiona said. "Trouble in Corn Pop world."

Over by the swing set, B.J. had her fists balled up as she took a step toward Anne-Stuart—whose hands were poised like feline claws as she met B.J. head-on.

"There's going to be a catfight," Darbie said.

Julia stood watching Anne-Stuart and B.J. with a smirk on her face, raking her thick hair back as if she wanted a better view.

"Do you think they're fighting over Jimmy?" Kitty said.

"I know they are."

For the second time in just a few days, Willoughby was suddenly there behind them, talking out of the side of her mouth like a ventriloquist. Fiona arched an eyebrow at her, but Darbie inched closer.

"So—tell us," she said.

Sophie had to admit she was interested too. They all gathered in as Willoughby whispered, "Julia told me that B.J. told her that she asked Jimmy to be her date at the dance, only Jimmy said no."

"Okay, he's way smarter than I thought," Fiona said.

"Then Julia told me that she told B.J. it was probably because Anne-Stuart already asked him. So B.J. got all mad and went looking for Anne-Stuart, only Anne-Stuart was already mad at B.J. because Jimmy told HER no, and she thought it was because B.J. already asked him, when she KNEW Anne-Stuart liked him."

"But didn't Anne-Stuart do the same thing to B.J.?" Sophie said.

"That's just the way they are," Willoughby said. "They do stuff like that to each other all the time. I don't even know why they're friends."

Fiona blinked at her. "So why are you friends with them?"

Willoughby switched the mouth hole to the other side of her face. "I'm thinking about not being friends with them anymore, only I have to find just the right way so they won't turn on me and make my life a total nightmare."

Sophie was about to nod when several shadows fell across them.

"Hi," Jimmy Wythe said.

Sophie stared up into his very blue eyes.

"This is where you say hi back," Willoughby whispered to her.

"Hi," Sophie said.

"What are they doing NOW?" said somebody else. It was Vincent. The other three boys were loitering behind them. The round-faced twins flapped their hands in a wave for a fraction of a second at Darbie and Willoughby. Nathan grinned at Kitty, flashing his braces, and then looked at the ground while his ears went crimson. Sophie was sure Kitty was going to pass out.

"They're fighting over you," Fiona said to Jimmy. "Go figure."

"Fiona!" Kitty said. "Rude!" Sophie glared at Fiona.

"That's okay—I don't get it either," Jimmy said. "They're like bees swarming around me all the time."

"You hate it then," Fiona said.

"Ya think?" Vincent said. His voice went from way-low to way-high and back again. "We had to stuff Jim in his locker just now because we heard them coming down the hall."

"No, you didn't," Fiona said.

"Yeah, we did. Ask these guys."

They all nodded.

"You are awesome," Fiona said. She put up her palm and Vincent high-fived it. Sophie could only stare.

"So," Vincent said, crossing his arms and tucking his hands into his armpits. "What is it you guys do when you're out here? Are you acting stuff out?"

Kitty giggled herself over to Nathan. Sophie expected to see the tips of his ears start smoking any minute.

"You promise you won't tease us?" Kitty said. She pointed her pert little nose up at him.

"We won't," Vincent said. "Unless you're cooking up ways to bug guys."

"We hate that," Ross and Ian said together.

"Are you insane?" Fiona said. "No—we're rehearsing for our next film. We do our own video productions, write the scripts and everything."

"What kind of video camera you got?" Ian said.

Sophie looked at Maggie, who knew all the numbers and letters that formed the answer to that, but Maggie was half-way behind Kitty, her eyebrows hooded over her cheekbones.

The bell rang, backpacks were hitched back up onto shoulders, and everyone moved toward the building.

"Are you going to be in social studies today?" Jimmy said. He was at Sophie's elbow. His voice was husky compared to the other boys, especially compared to the Fruit Loops who still sounded like girls.

Sophie was sure this was where she was supposed to say yes, but it was hard to get it out. The word squeaked through mouse-like.

"Are you?" she added.

Jimmy smiled his big white-toothed smile that went farther up one side of his face than it did on the other. "We're doing our culture presentation," he said.

"What's it about?" Sophie said.

"You'll see. It's a surprise—nobody knows except Ms. Quelling."

"Okay," Sophie said.

He smiled again, and then shrugged and said, "Well, I gotta go." And he hurried off to the same place she was going.

"I know why he said no to B.J. and Anne-Stuart." It was Willoughby—again.

"Because he doesn't like them?" Sophie said.

"Partly. And partly because he likes somebody else." Willoughby smiled as if she were completely pleased with herself and skipped on.

Sophie was left to stare after her. *It's like everybody was in all their right cubbyholes when I got up this morning,* she thought. *And then some giant came along and dumped them all out, and now nobody's where they were before.*

Uneasiness seeped in.

It's definitely something I'll have to keep my eye on, thought Agent Shadow. *Something like this could throw me off my focus, which isn't boys. Well, it's partly boys—but just the Fruit Loops Mob, who we must take down once and for all at the ball. THAT is our mission.*

The secret agent adjusted her special see-all glasses and swept her eyes across the hallway. That little wavy-haired girl would bear watching. There was still the possibility that she could be a spy for the Corn Pops Organization. Or connected with the Fruit Loops Mob.

And Agent Shadow must find out what had occurred that was driving Owl back into her shell. No matter how relationships seemed to be shuffling around, she had a job to do.

It was hard to concentrate on anything else but that job. She was so into Agent Shadow during language arts that she left the class at the end of the period not quite sure what Mr. Denton had just taught. But she was no closer to figuring out what was wrong with Maggie, who didn't answer the note Sophie had slipped to her on her way to the pencil sharpener. Toward the end of the class Maggie had gotten a bathroom pass and was gone for a long time.

Yet even Maggie faded into the background of Sophie's thoughts when Jimmy and his group entered the social studies room after class had started, ready for their presentation.

They were all dressed in black pants and white shirts with billowy sleeves and boots that went up to their knees. When they first dashed up to the front of the room, the Fruit Loops started to snicker—until one by one each boy in Jimmy's group pulled from his leather belt a real-looking sword, painted gold and gleaming in the sunlight through the window.

"Dude!" Colton said. "Are those real?"

"No! Now just watch," Ms. Quelling said.

She didn't have to tell anyone twice. For the next ten minutes the five boys—Vincent, Nathan, Ian, Ross, and Jimmy—swash-buckled back and forth across the front of the classroom, jumping up on Ms. Quelling's desk to engage in swordplay, clacking their weapons together, doing somersaults to avoid being run through. It was like watching a dance.

At the end there was a burst of applause, and Jimmy and his group took a bow, swishing their swords over their heads. Even the Fruit Loops whistled through their fingers and clapped like apes.

All the Corn Pops sat on top of their table, swaying and tossing their heads and looking at one another with bulging eyes.

"They're swooning," Fiona said to the Flakes.

"Look at Anne-Stuart," Darbie said. "She's all but hysterical, that girl."

By then B.J. was up on her knees, waving her hand, very obviously at Jimmy. Anne-Stuart leaned in front of her, flailing a tissue.

"I hope that's not used," Fiona said.

Sophie put her hand up to her mouth to stifle a giggle.

"Sophie!" Kitty whispered beside her. "He's looking at you!"

"Who?"

Darbie put a hand on each side of Sophie's head from the back and pointed it toward the line of musketeers at the front. Jimmy Wythe rose from his final bow and smiled his crooked smile at Sophie.

"He's not the only one looking," Fiona said. She jerked her head toward the Corn Pops' table, and Sophie heard Kitty gasp.

Not only Anne-Stuart and B.J., but Julia too stared at Sophie as if their very eyes were swords. Sophie could almost feel them slicing right into her brain, where they clearly left their message: *you will live to regret this.*

Eight

You need to watch your back, Soph," Fiona said after class.

"Better yet, we'll be watching it FOR you." Darbie's dark eyes narrowed. "It's going to take all of us—Fiona, me, Kitty, and Maggie."

"Where is Maggie?" Kitty said. "She went to the bathroom AGAIN last period, and she didn't come back."

Maggie didn't come to arts class either. When she didn't show up in the cafeteria, the Corn Flakes downed the contents of their lunch boxes and went to the office.

"Maggie's mother came and got her," the lady at the counter told them. "She wasn't feeling well."

"Was she throwing up?" Kitty said. "I hope not—that's the worst."

"Poor Mags," Darbie said.

The pixie-faced lady smiled. "I'm not sure what was wrong, but it's sweet that you girls are so concerned about your friend."

"Of COURSE we're concerned," Sophie said. "She's one of us."

"We still need to practice if we're ever going to get this film done," Fiona said as they hurried out to the playground.

Sophie nodded in a vague way. *Why would Maggie leave school without telling us?* she thought. *That's not the Corn Flake way.*

When they got to their place by the fence, Fiona said, "Let's set up the scene. Kitty, you stand over there and pretend you're powdering your nose, only you're really looking behind you in the little mirror. Then—"

"There they go," Darbie said, pointing. "Acting the eejit again."

They all glanced nearby where Anne-Stuart and B.J. were walking backward. Fiona groaned. "Their picture is next to 'acting the eejit' in the dictionary," she said in a low voice.

Sophie had to agree that the Corn Pops—at least, Anne-Stuart and B.J.—were putting on their worst display yet. They were walking backward to face Jimmy and Vincent, who both were looking over their heads, down at their toes, everywhere but at the two girls.

"You were SO awesome with that sword," Sophie heard Anne-Stuart say.

"You made it look, like, so REAL," B.J. said, placing her shoulder in front of Anne-Stuart's. "My heart was beating, like, ninety miles an hour."

Anne-Stuart replaced B.J.'s shoulder with her own. "It was the best sword fighting I ever saw. You were, like, professional."

"Like she knows so much about swordplay," Darbie muttered.

"They're acting like Vincent wasn't even there!" Fiona whispered. "They're just totally blowing him off."

At that exact moment, B.J. wedged her way between the two boys, putting her back in Vincent's face and elbowing him out of the conversation.

"That's totally heinous!" Fiona hissed.

Kitty went wide-eyed as she looked at Fiona. "You LIKE Vincent, don't you!" she said into Fiona's ear.

"Shhh! They'll hear!" Sophie whispered.

Fiona was shaking her head hard. "I mean, I like him," she hissed at Kitty, "but not like a boyfriend or something. I just think they're being jerks to him."

Vincent didn't look that hurt to Sophie. He stopped long enough to keep B.J. from stepping on him in her attempt to snatch Jimmy away from the hold Anne-Stuart had on his other arm. Then he grabbed the back of Jimmy's T-shirt and dragged him around the two girls and away from both of them.

"Hello! Rude!" B.J. shouted after him.

"HE's rude?" Fiona whispered. "What about THEM?"

Again, it didn't seem to bother Vincent. In fact, he didn't look back as he steered Jimmy the ten steps to the Corn Flakes. Sophie looked behind her to see if Nathan or the twins were there waiting for him, but there was only the fence. When she turned back, Jimmy and Vincent had stopped just in front of her. The two Corn Pops, of course, were so close behind them they nearly ran up the two boys' calves.

B.J. whipped off the hooded shirt she had tied around her waist and wrapped it around Jimmy's chest from behind, using the sleeves to tug him backward.

"You're not getting away that easy!" she said. She had her chin tucked in and her eyes slanted down. To Sophie, she looked like a cat with a mouse in its claws.

Jimmy, who up to that point had been looking bewildered, lifted both his arms and wiggled from B.J.'s trap. When Anne-Stuart leaped in front of him, he said, "Vincent and I need to talk to Sophie and Fiona."

"So talk," Anne-Stuart said, with the usual sniff.

"In private," Jimmy said.

Behind him, B.J.'s shoulders sagged until they almost met over her chest. Anne-Stuart looked over her own shoulder at the Corn Flakes as if she were only now noticing they were there—and wishing they weren't.

You will live to regret this was once more carved into her face.

"Okay," B.J. said, lower lip hanging down over her chin. "We'll just wait for you."

"What part of 'no' don't you understand?" Vincent said.

"Are you the boss of Jimmy?" B.J. shot back.

Vincent gave her a slow, sloppy smile. "Well, you sure aren't."

Jimmy stepped around Anne-Stuart and looked down at Sophie. There was a pink spot at the top of each cheekbone, and his eyes were shy.

"Can Vincent and I talk to you and Fiona?" he said. He glanced up at Darbie and Kitty, who were openly staring without apology. "I don't mean to be rude—"

"No worries," Darbie said. She jerked her head from Kitty to the two Corn Pops with a splash of hair. "We'll be sure you have some space."

With that she stepped between Anne-Stuart and B.J., dragging a less enthusiastic Kitty by the sleeve, and said, "We would love to talk to YOU privately."

Remember the Corn Flake rules, Sophie wanted to call after them as Darbie and Kitty herded them away. There was no telling what might come out of Darbie's mouth if she got good and mad. It could get ugly.

Vincent folded his arms, hands in his pits again, and said, "We wanna ask you something."

"If it's what I think it is," Fiona said, "we don't think you should choose either B.J. OR Anne-Stuart, Jimmy."

"Excuse me?" Jimmy said.

"That's not the question," Vincent said. His voice crackled.

Jimmy gave a soft grunt. "Are you kidding me? They're stalking me." He held up five fingers. "That's how many times B.J. called me last night. My mom finally told her not to do it again—it was, like, nine thirty."

"How many times did Anne-Stuart call?" Fiona said.

"She didn't. She emailed me. Six times."

"Big throw-up," Fiona said. She turned to Vincent. "They're absolutely horrific to you."

He gave an I-don't-care shrug. "This morning Julia comes up to me like she wants to be best friends or something, and then she asks me which one Jimmy likes better—Anne-Stuart or B.J."

"No way," Fiona said. "What did you say?"

"I told her he liked them both the same, which was not at all."

"I bet she didn't like that answer."

"No. She tried to pull my nose off."

"Are you SERIOUS?" Sophie said.

"Check it out." Vincent displayed his profile. "It's, like, an inch longer now."

He grinned, and so did Jimmy.

"That's just WRONG," Fiona said. She looked at Sophie, and they both dissolved into giggles.

"I didn't tell her this," Vincent said, "'cause she might go after my ears next, but Jimmy would rather be tortured than go to the dance with either one of them, even though they asked him about four times apiece."

Jimmy raised five fingers again.

"Nuh-uh!" Fiona said.

He nodded and grinned, and then the pink spots turned to red. He drew a line in the dirt with his heel. Vincent jabbed him with an elbow.

"There's only one person I want to be at the dance with," Jimmy said to the ground. He looked up at Sophie, the red spots covering the sides of his face. "And that's you."

"And I want to go with you," Vincent said to Fiona. "Only I don't dance that good."

"If you're coordinated enough to do stage combat, you can dance," Fiona said. "I can show you some stuff my grandfather taught me—it's not that hard."

"So—is that a yes?" Vincent said.

"Ye—" Fiona stared to say. But she stopped and looked at Sophie.

Sophie herself was gaping at Fiona, chin to her chest. Her heart was racing, and she knew the red places in her own face were starting to match the ones on Jimmy's.

She's acting like boys ask us out every day! she thought. *Doesn't she know what just happened? They invited US—not one of the pretty girls—not the popular ones that know what to do around boys. They asked US!*

"I'll only go with you if Sophie goes with Jimmy," Fiona said to Vincent.

All three faces turned to Sophie, but she saw only Jimmy's. His head was tilted to the side, and his forehead was folded into worried wrinkles. She could see that there was a smile waiting on the other side of that anxious expression, if only she said the right thing.

Darbie was right, Sophie thought. *I do feel special.*

She tilted her chin up. "Can you waltz?" she said to Jimmy.

"Are you KIDDING?" Vincent said. "He can do ANY dance."

Jimmy nodded. The smile was still waiting.

Sophie sucked in a big breath. "Then I accept," she said.

Jimmy grinned so big she was sure the corners of his mouth were going to disappear into his ears.

"Sweet." Vincent shuffled his feet as if he had run out of things to say, for Jimmy or himself. "We gotta go. See you in class."

"You know it," Fiona said.

The bell rang, and the two boys took off toward the building, bumping shoulders and slugging each other with lazy fists. As Fiona and Sophie headed in the same direction, Fiona clutched Sophie's arm.

"Pretend you don't see them staring at you," she said between gritted teeth.

"Who?"

"Who else?"

Sophie didn't have to look hard to see Anne-Stuart, B.J., and Julia gathered next to the trashcan that held the door open. All six eyes were trained on Sophie like shotgun barrels. But instead of dread, Sophie felt something else pulling her shoulders up straight.

"They're so jealous," Fiona said before they got within hearing range. "And you didn't even have to ask Jimmy—he asked you."

Sophie couldn't smother a grin as she turned her head toward the Pops.

Fiona gave her a rib poke. "But don't look at them! It's totally un-Corn-Flake-like to gloat."

So together they pretended to have important business to attend to on the other side of the door and zoned in on getting through. The Corn Pops didn't make a move—until Fiona went inside just ahead of Sophie.

Before Sophie could get her foot over the threshold, she felt her backpack coming off and something heavy slamming behind her. She tried to turn to the right to see, but she found herself being spun to the left by hurried hands.

Once. Twice. With faces blurring past. When the Corn Pops let go, Sophie staggered and hit the metal trashcan. Its lid clattered off, revealing the smell of rotten banana peels and the sight of Sophie's backpack half buried in garbage.

When she reached out to grab it, she heard Ms. Quelling's voice barking from the doorway.

"Sophie, why are you digging through the trash, child?"

"I'm getting my backpack," Sophie said. She yanked it loose and held it out at arm's length. Stuck to the corner was a wad of green gum. Stuck to the gum was a piece of paper.

"How did your backpack get in there?" Ms. Quelling said.

"You don't want to know," Sophie said.

"Fine. Now go wipe it off in the restroom before you go to class. Mrs. Utley is not going to appreciate that lovely aroma in her classroom." She scribbled out a hall pass on a pink pad and handed it to Sophie. "You are such a bizarre child. I think you're going to graduate from here without my ever figuring you out."

Sophie shook that comment off as she hurried to the girls' restroom, holding her backpack away from her with one hand while she pinched her nostrils with the other. The paper was still dangling from the wad of gum.

In the bathroom, she pulled it off with a paper-towel-covered hand and was about to deposit it, gum and all, in the trash can when something on the paper caught her eye. The writing looked familiar. Only Anne-Stuart made all those curlicues.

Sophie let the gum plop into the garbage can and shook out the wrinkled paper. It was Anne-Stuart's penmanship, all right, *and* her bad spelling.

Dear Julia,

B.J. is making me mad the way she is chaseing Jimmie. She knows I like him and that's the onley reason she's doing it. He dosen't like her and she's always hanging around me, so now he thinks I'm just like her and I'm SOOOO not!!!!!! Tod asked me to the dance and I'm going with him. It mite be kinda fun because you'll be with Colton. Du-uh! Everybody knows you're going out. I thot Jimme and I were going to be until B.J. I thot she was my friend, but your a much better one. She's not the onley one who is out to get me. Those freeks — Soapy and Fiona and them — their trying to get Jimmie away from me just to be hatefull. Like they can. Once he sees that Soapy is WEIRD, then he'll WISH he was with me. If that happens, I'll just break up with Tod.

LOL!! What if B.J. is the onley one of us who doesn't have a date at the dance!!!! I don't mean to be meen, but I think she deserves it.

TTFN,

Your best friend, Anne-Stuart

P.S. I know you won't tell BJ about any of this. We can't trust her. Just throw away this note after you read it.

P.P.S. After lunch I'm going to ask Jimmie one more time. Will you please keep B.J. out of my way?

Sophie dropped the note in the trash and went to the sink to scrub her hands.

Fiona would say that was the most heinous thing she ever read, Sophie thought. *Anne-Stuart's turning one of her friends against another one. And wishing her almost-best friend would be the only one without a boy to be with at the dance. How grotesque is that?*

She ripped some paper towels from the dispenser and went after a red juice stain on her backpack.

I can't even imagine doing that to one of my friends. We made a pact, sure, but we ALL broke it —

Except for Maggie.

Sophie froze and watched her face go pale in the mirror. Kitty and Nathan. Darbie and Ian. Fiona and Vincent. Herself and Jimmy.

Maggie and No One. Sophie left the water running as she turned away from the mirror. It was too hard to look at her own face. *We broke our promise to Maggie. We've left her out. We aren't any better than the Corn Pops.*

Sophie didn't know how long she had stood there leaning against the sink, chasing the same accusations around in her head, when the bathroom door swung open and Willoughby appeared.

"THERE you are!" she said. "Fiona is about to go nuts." She sniffed. "What stinks?"

"I do," Sophie said. "I'm disgusting."

Willoughby brought her nose closer to Sophie.

"No, it isn't you." She reached behind Sophie and held up Sophie's backpack. Water poured from one corner into a puddle on the floor. "It's this. It smells like garbage."

Sophie grabbed the backpack and whirled around to turn off the faucet. Water was creeping dangerously close to the top of the sink.

"I know who did this," Willoughby said.

"Me too," Sophie said.

"And I also know why."

"Me too."

Willoughby squinted her hazel eyes at Sophie. Two tiny lines formed between them.

"Aren't you mad?" she said.

"I'm mad at myself," Sophie said.

"Because of Maggie being the only one who hasn't been asked?"

Sophie felt her eyes bulge. "How did you know that?"

"I heard Fiona telling Darbie and Kitty just now."

"Now everybody's going to know what horrible friends we are!" Sophie could hear her own whine out-Kittying Kitty's.

"I'm not going to tell anybody," Willoughby said. "I swear."

Sophie dragged her backpack behind her, trailing water across the restroom. "I have to go talk to the Corn Fla—my friends."

She turned toward the door, but Willoughby caught her by the strap of her pack.

"There's one more thing you should know," she said. The two little lines were cutting into the bridge of her nose. "Maggie isn't just going to be the only one in your group who won't have a boy. She's the only one in the entire CLASS."

"What about Harley and—"

"Those girls aren't even going at all—they think it's lame—and B.J. just now asked Eddie, in case she can't get Jimmy to go with her."

"I'M going with him," Sophie said miserably. Just ten minutes ago that had made her feel special, like a princess. Now it was the very thing that made her want to escape into a bathroom stall for the rest of her life.

"B.J. doesn't know that yet," Willoughby said. She tucked her poodle hair behind her ears. "But when she does, she ISN'T going to be happy. Trust me."

Sophie wasn't sure she could trust Willoughby—but she definitely knew she was right. Too right.

Nine

✿ 🏠 ☀

"What are we going to do?" Sophie said when she and the Corn Flakes caught up between science and math. She was afraid she was going to start crying. Kitty already had.

"I don't think we should do anything until we have a plan," Fiona said. "Nobody call Maggie and tell her. We'll think of something by tomorrow."

"We should all pray about it," Darbie said. She looked at Kitty. "You can pray even if you don't go to church."

Sophie didn't feel a twinge this time. She felt a STAB. She still hadn't talked to Jesus.

I haven't told him one thing in days, she thought. *I wonder if he'll even listen to me right now. I can't just go back and start asking him for stuff now.*

For once, somebody else was going to have to come up with something. All Sophie could think of between then and the next morning was more heinous things about herself.

She was the one who had said Maggie was "one of us." And then ten minutes later she had told Jimmy she would go to the dance with him—and left Maggie sticking out like a sore toe.

She was the one who was always telling the girls they couldn't be un-Corn-Flake-like to the Corn Pops. But the minute some boy had made her feel special, she had forgotten about one of her own friends.

There's only one thing to do, she thought on the bus the next morning, *and that's tell Jimmy I can't go to the dance with him. I'll just hang out with Maggie—and we'll have even more fun.*

But in the next second she knew that wouldn't work. Fiona had said she would go with Vincent only if Sophie went with Jimmy. Sophie couldn't imagine doing that to Fiona, who had already arranged to give Vincent dancing lessons.

"You going to that Bible thing again?"

Sophie jumped. Gill was hanging over the seat in front of her, ball cap on backward.

"It's today," Gill said.

"Yeah," Sophie said. There was another stab. She had offered to take Maggie with her. What if Maggie wouldn't go now because Sophie didn't even act like a Christian—betraying her friend?

"I'm going," Gill said. "Me and Harley. I like that Dr. Peter guy."

"Me too," Sophie mumbled. That was the final stab: Dr. Peter was going to think she was the most awful person on the planet.

Fiona met Sophie as she dragged herself off the bus.

"You can lose the long face, Soph," she said. "Maggie's mom called Kitty to tell her to get Maggie's homework because she isn't coming to school today. That means we have more time to think of a plan. I have an idea." She looped her arm through Sophie's.

Sophie's heart lifted. *You decided not to go with Vincent?*

"I say we ask Dr. Peter about everything today in Bible study."

Sophie sagged. "In front of Harley and Gill?"

"They won't tell Maggie. Besides, the one I'm worried about is Willoughby. Have you noticed she's everywhere we are lately?"

Sophie nodded. Maybe Willoughby could come in and take her place and Sophie could just disappear.

Sophie felt heavier as the day went on, although Darbie and Fiona were counting the hours until it was time for Bible class. Sophie just knew Dr. Peter was going to be so disappointed in her—though not more disappointed than she was in herself. That wasn't possible.

"You okay, Dream Girl?" Mama said to her when the three of them climbed into the car after school.

Sophie suddenly wanted to pour it all out to her. She might be disappointed in Sophie too, but she was Mama. She still had to love her.

Dr. Peter had juice and a giant cookie for each of them when they arrived in the beanbag room. Sophie turned hers down.

"You're getting as bad as Maggie," Darbie said.

"I bet that's why she's sick," Fiona said. "She doesn't eat enough."

"I never have that problem." Gill looked wistfully at Sophie's uneaten cookie. "Can I have yours?"

"I feel stress in the air," Dr. Peter said as he pulled his red beanbag closer to the circle. "Anything you want to talk about?"

"We thought you'd never ask," Fiona said. She looked quickly at the two Wheaties, but Gill said, "Go for it."

Fiona picked right up where she'd left off the week before and filled Dr. Peter in. Sophie couldn't look at him. She didn't want to see herself falling from her place in his eyes.

He was quiet for a minute after Fiona was finished.

"Uh-oh," Fiona said. "Even you don't have an answer?"

"I have several," Dr. Peter said. Sophie didn't have to look to see that there was no twinkle on his face. "But this is one of those situations where it's going to make a lot more sense if you figure it out for yourselves."

"If we could do that, we would!" Darbie said. "We've been pounding our brains!"

"I didn't say I wasn't going to help you. I'm going to give you an assignment that I think is going to make it all very clear."

Sophie was glad she could keep her eyes on her Bible. But when Dr. Peter told them to imagine themselves in the story of the rich young man in Mark 10, and Sophie saw that Jesus was in it, she wanted to pull the whole beanbag over her head.

What if Jesus doesn't want me in his stories, the way I've been ignoring him lately? she thought.

"'As Jesus started on his way'" Dr. Peter read, "'a man ran up to him and fell on his knees before him. "Good teacher," he asked, "what must I do to inherit eternal life?"'"

"Does that mean go to heaven?" Fiona said.

"Basically, yes," Dr. Peter said.

"Gotcha. Go on."

Sophie imagined herself on her knees with Jesus looking right through her. If there was anybody who needed help getting to heaven, it was her right now.

"'Why do you call me good?" Jesus answered. "No one is good—except God alone.'"

That was kind of a relief, Sophie decided.

"'You know the commandments: "Do not murder, do not commit adultery, do not steal, do not give false testimony, do not defraud, honor your father and mother.'"

Sophie was pretty sure she hadn't broken any of those, even with Maggie. Still she bowed down even farther in front of Jesus. She couldn't feel this bad and not have disobeyed *some* rule.

Dr. Peter read on. " 'Teacher,' he declared, " 'all these I have kept since I was a boy.' Jesus looked at him and loved him. 'One thing you lack,' he said. 'Go, sell everything you have and give to the poor, and you will have treasure in heaven. Then come, follow me.' "

Fiona gave a long, low whistle.

"What?" Dr. Peter said.

"MY parents would go straight to you-know-where. They're all about their stuff."

"This guy was too—and, Fiona, we can talk about your parents later. For now, let's continue." Dr. Peter's eyes scanned the page. " 'At this the man's face fell. He went away sad, because he had great wealth.' "

Sophie had a hard time imagining herself slinking off sad. If there was one thing she *wasn't*, it was wealthy. She decided to stick around in her mind for the next part. Maybe she was supposed to be somebody else in the story.

" 'Jesus looked around and said to his disciples, "How hard it is for the rich to enter the kingdom of God!" The disciples were amazed at his words. But Jesus said again, "Children, how hard it is to enter the kingdom of God! It is easier for a camel to go through the eye of a needle than for a rich man to enter the kingdom of God." ' "

Sophie heard herself gasping as she and the disciples looked at one another in dismay. *A camel can't pass through the eye of a needle!* she thought. She knew her face was puzzled as she looked at Jesus.

" 'He said, "With man it is impossible to be saved, but not with God; all things are possible with God." ' "

Sophie waited at Jesus' knee for him to say something more, to explain how this would help her make things right with Maggie.

But Jesus drifted away, and Dr. Peter closed the Bible.

"No offense," Fiona said, "but that doesn't help."

"It will," Dr. Peter said, "if you do this assignment I'm going to give you." He passed out hot-pink sheets with some words and blanks on them. "I want you to take this home and see what happens. I think you'll be surprised by what you figure out."

"Can we work on it together?" Darbie said.

Dr. Peter wrinkled his glasses up on his nose, and for an awful moment Sophie wondered if he was so disappointed in all the Corn Flakes that he was going to tell them no—they had done enough together. But finally he nodded his head of spiky hair and said, "As long as all of you work to find the right answers."

There was no time to get together that night, so they promised to meet in the morning before school, and they called Kitty to join them. But when they arrived at their secret place backstage in the cafeteria, Maggie was already there.

"Mags!" Kitty said, throwing her arms around Maggie's neck. "Are you better?"

Maggie nodded, but to Sophie she looked worse than she had the last time she'd seen her. She had deep, dark circles under her eyes, and her mouth was in a grim little line. Fiona gave Sophie a look that read, *Do you think she already knows?*

But Maggie didn't say anything about the boys or the dance. In fact, she didn't say much at all. She just sat under an arch of tissue-paper flowers that the fifth grade had used for their spring festival and listened while the rest of the Corn Flakes talked about everything but what they had come to discuss.

The only time Maggie reacted to anything was when the voices of Eddie, Tod, and Colton echoed against the cafeteria walls as they charged through. Maggie scooted herself behind Kitty and buried her face in her knees.

"Today is not the day to bring up anything," Fiona said to Sophie and Darbie after Kitty had followed Maggie to the bathroom.

"She's still sick," Sophie said.

Darbie frowned. "All right—but we better be hoping nobody else tells her."

First period went smoothly, and they knew in second period the Corn Pops were giving their culture presentation, so there wouldn't be a chance for any of them to talk to Maggie. In fact, the Pops were so busy rearranging the room, they didn't even give the Flakes any deadly looks.

I guess they don't know about Jimmy yet either, Sophie thought. But that didn't make her feel any better. Just then she would have given up everything she owned if that made any sense for Maggie. *I hate hating myself!* she thought.

"We're going to demonstrate a folk dance the peasants in France used to do," Julia said to the class when all the chairs and tables had been pushed against the walls. "And everyone has to do the dance with us."

"Aw, man!" Gill said, above the groans of everybody else.

"Uh-oh," Fiona said.

Sophie nodded. She had forgotten Anne-Stuart's words until now: *We're going to make the whole class participate.*

"Line up with your partner as I call your names," Julia said. B.J. and Anne-Stuart stood in the middle of the room as if they were ready to enforce Julia's every word. Willoughby stayed at the edge, looking like she wished she'd never heard of any of them.

"Julia and Colton," Julia said.

Colton grinned and went to the spot B.J. pointed out to him.

"B.J. and Eddie. Willoughby and Ross."

So far there were no surprises, but Sophie held her breath. The rest could be worse than heinous.

"Kitty and Ian."

"What?" Kitty whined.

"Darbie and Vincent. Fiona and Nathan."

"She doesn't know as much as she thinks she does," Fiona muttered to Sophie as she went to join Nathan, with Kitty whimpering in their direction.

The Wheaties looked relieved as Julia paired Harley and another Wheatie, then Maggie and Gill. Maggie didn't look any way at all. She shuffled next to Gill, her eyes on the floor.

"Sophie and Tod. Anne-Stuart and Jimmy."

Sophie felt the two red spots burning into her cheeks, but she moved slowly toward Tod. She couldn't make any more trouble with Ms. Quelling. *As long as I don't have to touch him, I can do it*, she told herself.

"Take your partner's hand," Julia said. "And we'll call out the instructions while we do it."

Tod looked as if he would rather hold a deep-sea creature than Sophie's hand. She knew exactly how he felt, but under Ms. Quelling's stern glare, she let him grab the tips of her fingers as if they were jellyfish tentacles. A shiver went through her from head to toe.

Julia called out instructions, but it didn't do much good. B.J. hauled Eddie around anywhere she could get a vantage point to give hate looks to Anne-Stuart because she was dancing with Jimmy. Kitty whined like a terrier every time she passed Fiona, who was only trying to keep Nathan from stepping on her toes. Tod abandoned Sophie altogether and grabbed Anne-Stuart from Jimmy, which sent her into a sniffling tizzy that brought the whole thing to a halt.

Ms. Quelling switched off the CD player and folded her arms. "Fix it, Julia," she said. "Or I'm taking off points."

"All right," Julia said with a sigh. It was obvious she had been enjoying the entire mess. "Everybody get with the partner you're going to have at the graduation dance and we'll start over."

Sophie felt herself going cold. Everyone shifted around, including Jimmy, who slid into place beside Sophie. Nearby, Vincent found his way to Fiona. The Wheaties pulled together in a sulky trio.

Maggie was left standing alone. In a frozen second, her eyes swept the room and came back to Sophie.

"Maggie?" Sophie said.

But Maggie's face crumpled, and she ran for the doorway, knocking Eddie against a table as she went.

"Hey, watch it, wide load!" Eddie called after her.

"Close your cake trap, blackguard!" Darbie shouted at him.

Sophie and Fiona tore for the door, but Ms. Quelling beat them there.

"You stay right here," she said, her face twisted down at them. "I'll call the counselor."

Kitty burst into tears, and Fiona was barely able to hold Darbie back from poking Eddie's eyes out. Sophie could only stare out into the hallway where a shattered Maggie had disappeared.

I don't think SHE's the one who needs the counseling, Sophie thought. She wished with all her might for Dr. Peter—and some answers she could understand.

Ten

Fiona, Darbie, and Sophie were a long-faced, droopy group when they met in Sophie's family room that day after school to work on their Bible study assignment.

"I bet Willoughby was the one who told Julia about our dates for the dance," Fiona said. "I KNEW we couldn't trust her."

But Sophie shook her head. "It doesn't matter who told. We did a terrible thing to Maggie, and we have to take the blame for it."

"I hate it when you're right," Fiona said. She picked up her hot-pink sheet and put it down again. "No wonder Maggie can't eat if she feels like this."

Darbie opened her Bible and unfolded her sheet. "Come on then, enough. Dr. Peter says there's an answer in this Bible story, and we have to find out what it is before we all go mental."

"I just don't think it's in there," Fiona said.

But Sophie had been thinking about the Bible story ever since the dance disaster of second period. Every time Dr. Peter had given her a Jesus story to help her figure out a problem, it had always worked. Sometimes it just took a while to figure out.

"What does the sheet say to do?" she said.

Fiona picked it up again and scowled at it. "It says to answer the question next to each verse below and do, for real, what our answer says."

Darbie craned her neck over Fiona's shoulder. "Mark ten, verse seventeen. 'How did the rich young man get to Jesus?'"

"He ran to him," Fiona said, tapping the page with her eraser. "So — we run to Jesus. But he's not here."

"You imagine he is, in your mind," Sophie said. "That's what I do. Or at least, I used to, before I became a heinous person."

"Can you ever lay off that?" Darbie said. "Jesus already said God's the only one who's good — it says so right here — and he shows us how to be good. That's what we're getting back to. Now get off yourself and let's move on."

Sophie blinked. "So I can still run to him, you think?"

"If YOU can't, nobody can," Fiona said. "You're, like, perfect." She examined the sheet again. "Okay, what does he do when he gets to Jesus?"

"Falls on his knees," Sophie said.

"Then we need to be doing that right now," Darbie said. "We always act everything else out, don't we?"

Fiona was the first one in a kneeling position, sheet and Bible on the floor in front of her, pencil poised. Sophie closed her eyes.

"'What are three things he tells the man that are important?'" Fiona read.

Darbie paused for only a couple of seconds. "Only God is truly good. Know the commandments. Keep the commandments."

"Check," Fiona said. "So far, we already do all this stuff."

"Go on," Sophie said. She kept her eyes closed. Jesus was becoming clearer and her hands, for some reason, were getting sweaty, the way they did when Daddy was about to ground her for an impossibly long time.

"'What did Jesus tell him was the one reason he couldn't get eternal life?'" Fiona read.

"He cared too much about money," Darbie said.

"Wait—there's more." Fiona frowned at the directions. "'HINT: what is separating you from loving God more than anything else? It doesn't have to be money.'"

"Oh!" Darbie said. She had that light-bulb-over-the-head look. "The first day Dr. Peter said we would know it was our time for boys if they didn't get between us and God."

"Anne-Stuart and B.J. are the ones who practically knock each other out trying to get to Jimmy," Fiona said. "They DEFINITELY aren't thinking about God!"

"Today when Julia mixed all the couples up, just to be a control freak," Darbie said. "That wasn't about Jesus."

Sophie didn't say anything. She just looked down at her sweat-sparkly palms.

"What, Soph?" Fiona said. "You don't look so good."

"I think it's talking about ME!" Sophie sank back onto her feet and scrubbed her hands on her thighs. "I used to talk to Jesus all the time, but ever since this whole dance thing started I hardly go him at ALL. He must think I forgot all about him, because I'm always thinking about Kitty all giggling over Nathan, and Darbie feeling special for the first time because Ian asked her, and what to tell Maggie because Vincent and Jimmy asked you and me—"

"Mercy," said a voice in the doorway. "It sounds like a soap opera in here!"

Darbie's aunt Emily bustled into the room with Mama behind her. They perched on the edge of the couch.

"What's wrong?" Fiona said. "You look like we're busted."

"No, you aren't busted," Mama said. "We're just—concerned."

Aunt Emily pulled at a gold hoop earring. "Is your entire class pairing up for this dance?"

"Everybody but the Wheaties," Fiona said. "They aren't even going."

"And Maggie," Darbie said.

Sophie looked down at her hands, but she could feel Mama's eyes on her.

"I see," Mama said, dragging out the "I."

"That's exactly why kids your age are too young for the dating thing," Aunt Emily said. "Somebody gets left out—people get their feelings hurt."

"It isn't exactly a date," Fiona said.

"It might as well be," Mama said. She crossed her arms and drummed her fingers on the opposite arms. "I thought this dance was a bad idea for sixth graders to begin with, but I thought, well, you're so excited about the dresses, and you'll all go together and it will just be a girl thing."

"But it's not turning out that way." Aunt Emily looked at Mama, and they exchanged motherly looks. "I need to talk to Patrick."

"I know what my husband's going to say." Mama turned to the girls. "For right now, let's put your plans on hold."

Fiona had crawled up onto a chair and now stood on her knees. "What does that mean?"

"It means we're going to do what's healthy for you girls," Mama said. She put up her hand. "I know you, Fiona, and I don't want to hear your twenty arguments right now. You can save those for your Boppa."

"Boppa's too busy giving dumb flowers to Miss Odetta Clide," Fiona said when Mama and Aunt Emily had gone back to the kitchen. "He won't care that the Corn Pops AND the

Fruit Loops are going to hate us worse than ever if the dance gets called off."

"The Corn Pops?" Darbie said. "What about our Kitty?"

"There's only one person who might be happy about this," Fiona said, "and that's Maggie." She tried a smile that didn't work. "Maybe this solves our problem, huh?"

Sophie didn't even *try* to smile. "Maggie already knows we forgot all about her when we said we'd go to the dance with boys," she said. "I bet that hurts her more than the Fruit Loops calling her fat."

Their silence said they knew she was right again.

Between that and the fact that Darbie was right too—Kitty was going to dissolve into a puddle for sure if she didn't get to meet Nathan at the dance and act like he was her boyfriend—the girls were very down when they left Sophie's house.

Sophie didn't have any highs to tell at the supper table that night. When she tried to give a low, she had so much trouble picking just one that she burst into tears and excused herself from the table.

"Was it something I said?" she heard Daddy ask as she ran to her room.

No, she wanted to cry out, *it was something I said! I said yes, and it messed everything up!*

She had almost stopped "keening" over that, as Darbie would say, when Mama tapped lightly on her door. Sophie *really* didn't want to talk to her, but Mama only said, "Come downstairs. We have a visitor."

Sophie followed Mama down the steps with her heart dragging to her knees.

Senora LaQuita was in the family room, letting a mug of tea get cold on the coffee table in front of her. Mama ushered

Sophie to the chair across from her, and Daddy came in behind her, blocking all hope of escape.

"Senora LaQuita has been telling us why Maggie has been absent from school," Mama said.

For a tiny second, Sophie felt relieved. At least this wasn't about the dance.

"She never eat," Senora LaQuita said. "She say the boys, they call her fat."

Sophie's heart dropped.

"I didn't think it was like Maggie to pay attention to them," Mama said.

Daddy nodded. "She's usually such a little toughie."

Senora LaQuita shook her head, her turquoise earrings jittering against her face. "Never before. But now—the dance—boy asking girl. Now Maggie—she is very upset."

Sophie felt the tears fighting to get out again. "I'm SOOOO sorry!" she said. "I didn't want her to get all hurt like this! We promised her we would all go together, and then boys started asking—and I never thought one would ask me—and when he did I forgot about Maggie because I felt special, and so did Darbie and Fiona, and now I feel like the most heinous person in the world!"

Daddy shook his head a few fast times and crossed his eyes before he said, "Soph, that's not the point. This just confirms what your mother was saying to you earlier—this idea of a dance where boys can ask girls is too much for sixth graders. It isn't your fault that Maggie didn't get asked—but none of this would have happened if the school hadn't put you all in this position in the first place."

Senora LaQuita nodded sadly.

"We're going to talk to the other parents about this thing," Daddy said.

Mama put an arm around Maggie's mom's shoulder. "Meanwhile, we're going to postpone the fittings and give Señora LaQuita time to spend with Maggie."

"She's going to be okay, isn't she?" Sophie said.

"Doctor say she must eat," Maggie's mother said. "Margarita, she is—" She looked at the ceiling as if she were searching for the right word.

"Stubborn?" Daddy said.

Sophie leaned forward, clutching the edge of the coffee table. "We'll make her eat at school," she said, voice squeaking. "And we'll keep telling her she isn't fat."

"Sophie," Mama said. Her eyes were soft. "You aren't to blame that this is happening to Maggie. Just let her know you love her, that's all."

I can do that, Sophie thought as she trudged back up the stairs, *but I don't think she'll believe me.*

Maggie was absent again the next day, and Ms. Quelling told the Corn Flakes she'd been told that Maggie was going to be out the rest of the week.

"Has she helped you with your presentation?" she said. "She's not going to be here tomorrow when you do it."

"She got all the recipes for us and she and her mom gave us the ingredients they have at home and she would be here if she could." Sophie took a breath and added, "Ma'am."

"I'm convinced already," Ms. Quelling said. "Sophie, you really ought to consider switching to decaf."

Sophie could almost hear Maggie saying in her matter-of-fact voice, *Sophie doesn't even drink coffee*. Tears sprang to her eyes—yet again.

"Miss Odetta said we could cook at my house tonight," Fiona said when Ms. Quelling had left them alone. "We'll make killer enchiladas and get an A-plus for Maggie."

Then they slumped over their textbooks, and Sophie could see them all trying hard not to cry.

Mama and Daddy dropped Sophie off at Fiona's that night and picked up Boppa and Fiona's mom and dad. That's when she found out the sixth-grade parents were having a meeting at Anna's Pizza.

"They're talking to ALL the parents?" Sophie wailed when they'd left. "I thought just OURS were gonna decide if we could go!"

"We're doomed," Fiona said. She started slapping corn tortillas into a long glass dish.

Darbie went behind her, splattering spoonfuls of sauce into them. "If the Pops' parents are there, don't be surprised if we all have live snakes in our lockers tomorrow."

"I don't care about snakes or lockers," Kitty said. "I just want to go to the dance with Nathan!" She slammed a knife across a tomato, squirting seeds all the way to the refrigerator door.

Miss Odetta Clide was suddenly there, and she calmly took the blade from Kitty's hand. "This food will not be fit to eat if you don't stop attacking it," she said. "A lady does not mutilate her ingredients." She eyed the cheese Sophie was shredding into powder. "In fact, the preparation of a meal can be rather soothing to the soul. Now, shall we start again? Our cooking must be like a dance."

I'm starting to REALLY not like that word, Sophie thought.

She tried not to get into Miss Odetta Clide's rhythm as the old nanny floated the tortillas into the dish and poured the sauce, velvet-like, on them. The girls at first only followed her to mock her swirling hand movements and foot glides. But when she put on a collection of waltz music and refused to let them get by with any more slapping and splattering and slamming, lest there be demerits, they eased into the "dance" in spite of themselves.

In the end, they had twenty enchiladas that would have made Senora LaQuita herself proud.

"I bet Maggie would eat one of THESE," Fiona said.

"I wish she was going to be there," Kitty said.

Miss Odetta Clide made that clicking sound with her tongue. "A lady does not wish for things—at least not a lady of faith. She prays for them."

"Dr. Peter SAID we were supposed to get closer to God," Darbie said.

But Sophie was staring at Miss Odetta Clide. Fiona skipped staring and went straight to, "You pray?"

Miss Odetta's eyes seemed to slide right down her nose at Fiona. "Is that such a surprise?"

Nobody said anything.

"I pray every night that your brother and sister will not destroy each other before morning."

She's better than most of their nannies then, Sophie thought. *I bet the last four prayed that they WOULD.*

"I guess it's working," Fiona said. "Rory and Izzy are both still alive. Unfortunately."

"I also pray that you, Fiona, will develop a sweeter nature when it comes to your siblings."

"I'm going to start praying for that for my sister," Sophie said.

Miss Odetta Clide nodded. "There is nothing so small that we can't go to the Lord with it. And this situation with Margarita is actually quite large. An eating disorder can be difficult to control once it gets started."

"We'd better get praying then," Darbie said.

She put out her hands and the others latched onto her and one another—except Sophie. Her arms felt too heavy to lift.

"What's up, Soph?" Fiona said.

"I don't know," Sophie said. But she did. She felt so far away from Jesus, she couldn't even get him into her mind.

"If you don't pray, we're really doomed," Fiona said. "God ALWAYS listens to you."

Sophie felt herself caving in like a wet sandcastle. She wasn't sure what she would have said if they hadn't heard the front door open. The Corn Flakes all tore out of the kitchen, and even Miss Odetta Clide moved more briskly than usual.

Mama and Daddy, Boppa, and Fiona's tall, polished parents were all in the entrance hall, smelling like pepperoni and looking as if they'd just been pinched.

"So—what happened?" Fiona said, instead of "Hello."

Everybody looked at Daddy. "Some of us are going to the principal," he said. He pulled his mouth into a tight line. "And some of us aren't. It's still up in the air whether the dance will happen."

"Whether it will HAPPEN?" Kitty was giving new meaning to the word *whine*. "I thought you were just gonna talk about whether we could go with boys!"

"You mean it could get CANCELLED?" Darbie said.

"We're doomed," Fiona said for the third time that night. She looked at Sophie. "We should have prayed sooner."

Nobody had to tell Sophie that. *And now I bet it's too late*, she thought. With every passing second, she felt Jesus slipping farther away.

The next morning, the Corn Flakes, minus Maggie, met under the tissue-flower arch backstage.

"Who spied on parents when you got home last night?" Fiona said.

She, Darbie, and Kitty all raised their hands. Sophie shook her head. She hadn't WANTED to hear any more.

"Some of the parents still think the dance is okay," Kitty said. "Not MINE, though. I hate this!"

"I heard Aunt Emily say that Julia's mom threatened to call the superintendent if the dance was called off," Darbie said.

Fiona grunted. "Figures."

"I hope she does!" Kitty said. "I want to GO!"

Sophie forced herself not to put her hands over her ears. "We're not supposed to talk at school about this whole thing. That's what Mama and Daddy told me ALL the parents agreed on last night."

"Mine too," Darbie said.

Fiona looked as if she tasted something sour. "Most of the time mine barely know I GO to school, and now all of a sudden they're marching to the principal's office."

"But what if B.J. and the Pops know something we don't?" Kitty said.

"We're secret agents, aren't we?" Fiona said. "Nobody said we couldn't listen."

It became obvious the minute first period started that the Corn Pops' and Fruit Loops' parents hadn't told their kids to keep THEIR mouths shut about the dance.

Sophie got a note signed by all the Corn Pops before Mr. Denton had even taken the roll, saying, *Thanks for ruining everything, Soapy.*

The Fruit Loops knocked the Corn Flakes' books off their desks every time they went to the pencil sharpener or the bookshelf, which was every other minute.

After class, Eddie and Colton blocked the doorway to Ms. Quelling's room until the bell rang and made the Corn Flakes late for their own presentation. When they passed out the enchiladas, Julia, B.J., and Anne-Stuart went one by one to the trash can when Ms. Quelling wasn't looking and threw them away, paper plates and all. They made sure the Corn Flakes, however, couldn't miss it.

But it was Kitty who got to Sophie the most. At lunchtime, she didn't show up until long after the other Corn Flakes had already started eating their sandwiches, and when she did, she was quiet and stiff. After taking two bites of tuna salad, she said she didn't feel like rehearsing for their film and left the table to go to the library instead.

"What's up with HER now?" Fiona said.

"Maybe she's just worried about Maggie," Sophie said. "I don't feel that much like practicing either."

"Let's just sit here," Darbie said. "I don't have the heart for it without our Maggie."

"I know what's going on with Kitty." Of course it was Willoughby, sliding into the spot Kitty had just vacated. Her hazel eyes were shiny.

"Don't you think you've spread enough bad information?" Fiona said.

"Excuse me?"

"Nobody can tell whose side you're on anymore." Fiona's nostrils flared. "No thanks—we'll figure Kitty out for ourselves."

"That's fine with me," Willoughby said.

But Sophie could tell by the sting in Willoughby's eyes that it really wasn't fine.

"You were kind of rude to her, weren't you?" Sophie said to Fiona when Willoughby was gone.

"We just can't trust ANYBODY right now," Fiona said. "Just us—that's all. You know what?" She shot up from the table. "I can't sit here. Let's go outside."

They were gathered in a glum knot by their fence with nothing to say when they heard a husky voice clearing its throat. Sophie squinted through her glasses to see Jimmy, with Vincent, Nathan, Ian, and Ross.

"Everybody's dissing you," Jimmy said. His hands were shoved in his pockets, and his eyes dipped at the corners.

"So what else is new?" Fiona said.

Sophie looked at her quickly. Her face was as sharp as her voice.

"Yeah, but I heard they're planning something really bad now," Vincent said.

"We're here to offer our protection," Jimmy said. The guys behind him all nodded.

"Yeah, well, thanks," Fiona said. "But we—"

"Would really appreciate that!" Sophie said.

Fiona gave her a what-are-you-thinking glare.

"There are only three of us right now," Sophie said. "We need all the help we can get."

Fiona sighed. "So what are you going to do, come out here every lunch period and watch us rehearse for our film? That could get pretty boring."

Jimmy shrugged. "You got any roles for guys?"

"We usually play those," Fiona said.

"You COULD be, like, the federal agents we turn the mob over to when we get them. Or you could be counterspies when we write the script," Sophie said. "We're the secret agents."

"Sweet," Vincent said. "I have some walkie-talkies. I'll bring them."

"Before school," Sophie said. "We're gonna get here early to practice."

"We'll be here at zero-dark-thirty," Jimmy said.

Fiona gritted her teeth and said nothing. When the bell rang, she waited for the boys and Darbie to get ahead of them, and then strapped her fingers around Sophie's arm.

"What are you doing?" she said.

"We might need the protection," Sophie said. "You heard Vincent—if the dance gets called off, something really bad could happen to us."

Fiona sniffed through her flared-out nostrils. "We've always been able to handle the Corn Pops before—AND the Fruit Loops—all by ourselves."

"They never had this big of a reason to hate us before," Sophie said.

Eleven

In science class, Sophie watched, a lump swelling in her throat, as Kitty hunkered without a word over the chapter on bacteria. It was as if she was looking for the cure for some rare disease, and it didn't fit Canary's profile. Agent Shadow would have pointed that out if Sophie hadn't been too stuck to go into spy world.

"Kitty," Mrs. Utley said, a tease playing around her lips, "you feeling all right?"

Darbie and Fiona both gave hopeful laughs. Sophie just held her breath.

"I'm fine," Kitty said in a quivery voice. "Can I go to the restroom, please?"

Sophie could see her squeezing back tears until Mrs. Utley wrote out a pass and Kitty bolted out with it balled up in her fist.

"I'd hate to see her when she isn't fine," Fiona said.

Darbie flicked her eyes toward the Corn Pop table. "I bet it's one of them."

"Why wouldn't she tell us then?" Fiona said.

"Because we can't be trusted."

Fiona and Darbie stared at Sophie. "What are you saying?" Darbie said.

Sophie looked at Maggie's empty chair, the lump now potato-sized in her throat.

Fiona gave a long, ragged sigh. "I wish you'd get off that, Soph. We didn't mean to leave Maggie out. I want to tell her I'm sorry—but you're flagellating yourself."

Sophie felt her face going hot. "For once, would you talk like a sixth grader?"

Fiona's neck rose up out of her hunched shoulders. "Excuse me?" she said.

"She doesn't know what 'flagellating' means." Darbie's eyes shifted from one of them to the other. "It's like you're beating yourself with a stick, Sophie."

"She didn't have to be so rude about it," Fiona said.

"I'm not being rude!" Sophie knew her voice was squeaking. "Everything's confusing enough as it is, and you're just making it harder."

"Actually, now that I think about it—you're the one who's made it all harder."

"ME?"

"Well, no, not you—your parents. The dance would still definitely be happening it if weren't for them. Maybe Kitty IS mad at you—about THAT."

Sophie's mouth dropped open. "Boppa and your parents feel the same way!"

"So do mine," Darbie said. "Only—"

"Only what?" Sophie watched Darbie sweep the tabletop with her hand.

"Only, your mum and dad DID start it. I don't like Maggie being hurt either, but does that mean I have to give up something that's special to me? I wasn't the one who did it to her."

"Me either," Fiona said. "This is the first time I ever got excited about a DRESS. And I already started giving Vincent bop lessons!"

Sophie stared at them, mouth still open. What had just happened?

"Ladies." Mrs. Utley's chins were wobbling above them. "I thought you weren't in the crazy half."

"I think the whole class has gone mental," Darbie said to her.

"If you're going to go down with them," Mrs. Utley said, "just discuss it AFTER you've finished your assignment, all right?"

Who am I going to discuss it with? Sophie thought. *Who's left that understands?*

Darbie and Fiona went back to their work, stiff as sticks. Kitty returned from the restroom, with her eyes puffy and her face blotchy, just before the bell rang, and when it did, she didn't give the Flakes a chance to corner her. She fled as if she had a pack of wild dogs after her.

I might know how she feels, Sophie thought. She mumbled something to Darbie and Fiona about having to catch the bus and hurried for the front door, but when she got outside, Mama was there, standing in a patch of sunlight talking to the principal.

Sophie froze. Even when somebody poked her in the spine, she barely flinched.

"Why does your mother have to stick her nose into our business?" said a hot-breathed voice into her ear.

I don't know, Sophie wanted to say to B.J. *I don't know anything.*

B.J. suddenly jerked her hand up and called out, "Hi, Mrs. Olinghouse!"

The principal gave an automatic smile, said something in a low tone to Mama, and strode off toward the buses. Mama held out her hand to Sophie.

I hope she doesn't start in, Sophie thought. *I already yelled at Fiona, which is bad enough.* She wasn't sure she could hold back with her mother—and Mama had grounding power.

Maybe I should just be grounded for life, she thought to herself. *Then I wouldn't be messing things up all the time.* She could barely drag one foot after the other as she went to her.

"Did you forget that this was your day with Dr. Peter?" Mama said.

Sophie had, and now that Mama was leading her toward the old Suburban, she wasn't sure how to feel. Dr. Peter was the perfect person to talk this out with, but if he was disappointed in her, she wasn't sure she could stand it.

She was still trying to decide when she followed him into his room. But after one look at his eyes searching hers from behind his glasses when they sat down on the window seat, she blurted out everything as if she were avoiding torture. The whole time, she was searching *his* eyes for glints of disappointment.

There weren't any. Instead, he ran his hand across the top of his spiky curls. "This is a tough one, Loodle," he said. "What is Jesus saying about it?"

Sophie wanted to plaster one of the pillows on her face. "Nothing."

"Because—"

"Because I haven't been talking to him."

"Because—"

There were suddenly tears to be blinked away. "Because I don't think I can go to him now!" she said. "I've been away from him so long, he won't want to hear me anymore!"

Dr. Peter handed her a tissue and waited while she blew her nose. She was feeling as drippy as Anne-Stuart. Dr. Peter leaned toward her with firm eyes.

"Listen to me carefully," he said. "God is ALWAYS there for you, no matter how long it's been since you even thought about him. Jesus is the way to him, and that way is always available. Are we clear?"

"No," Sophie said.

"Why not?"

"Because I can't make myself go back to him. I'm too ashamed."

She needed another tissue then.

"Did you and the Corn Flakes do your assignment?" Dr. Peter said.

Sophie nodded.

"And did you figure out what stands between you and God? Because that's what this whole thing is about, you know. Something is getting in the way."

"It isn't money, like that guy in the story," Sophie said. "And it isn't Agent Shadow—even being her doesn't make me feel any better."

"New film character?" Dr. Peter said.

"Yes."

"Secret Agent?"

"Uh-huh."

"Let's investigate a little further then." Dr. Peter scrunched his neck down and looked over his shoulders as if at that very moment someone might be spying on them. After humming a few bars of the *Mission Impossible* theme, he said, "My sources tell me that a number of things can get between a girl and God—"

He started ticking off his fingers. "Popularity?"

"No."

"Grades?"

"Nope."

"Parents?"

"Not anymore."

"Fashion?"

Sophie looked down at her nearest-thing-to-Colonial-style skirt that no Corn Pop would be caught DEAD in. "I don't THINK so!" she said.

"Boys?"

Sophie hesitated, but then she shook her head. Boys might have gotten between her and Maggie, but they didn't separate her from God.

Dr. Peter pulled all his fingers back in. "Then I think there's only one answer, Agent Loodle. The thing that's keeping you from going to Jesus—is you."

"ME?!"

"I think Jesus wants to say to you, 'Sophie, leave behind all your mistakes and your shame and just hang out with me.'" He shrugged. "He's probably tried to tell you that himself, only you weren't listening."

"I'm standing in my own way?" Sophie said.

Dr. Peter lowered his voice. "Let me tell you a little agent secret: most of the people who come to see me are doing that."

Sophie looked down at the tissue and tore a hunk out of it. "I don't know how to stop doing it."

"You've come to the right place," Dr. Peter said. "It's really pretty easy. You just need to stop believing that you have to be close to perfect before you can talk to Jesus."

"You don't think he's disappointed in me?" Sophie said.

"He's already forgiven you because he loves you. Love is always where it starts with God. Now you have to accept that and get back to talking to him."

"Like now?"

"That would be good, yeah."

Sophie bowed her head, but then she looked up at Dr. Peter again.

"Do you think you could come with me?" she said.

"Sure, I can put in a good word for you." Dr. Peter folded his hands. "Shall we?"

As he prayed, Sophie had never seen Jesus more clearly in her mind. His eyes were kinder than ever, and when she asked him—okay, begged him—to show her what she was supposed to do about her Corn Flakes, she felt a little inkling of hope.

Sophie was transporting the salad dressing bottles from the table back to the refrigerator after supper when the phone rang. Daddy answered it, said "Uh-huh" a couple of times, and hung up, jaw muscles twitching.

"Mrs. Olinghouse?" Mama said.

"Lacie," Daddy said, "why don't you take Zeke upstairs?"

"Busted," Lacie murmured to Sophie as she steered Zeke toward the door. The potato lump reformed in Sophie's throat.

"What did she tell you?" Mama said to Daddy.

"She said she appreciated us all coming in to talk to her today, and that she understood our concerns, but—"

"They're going to go ahead with the dance," Mama finished for him.

"You got it."

They both turned to Sophie, but before they could even get their mouths around their words, Sophie said, "It doesn't matter. I'm not going."

Their eyebrows lifted as if they were pulled up by the same string. But neither one of them seemed as surprised as she was.

I don't know where that came from! Sophie thought. *Was that Agent Shadow talking?*

No—this decision could ruin the whole film and maybe even push the Corn Flakes further away from her.

But it might also show Maggie that Sophie loved her more than a dress or a date—and that was where it had to start. If Dr. Peter was right, love was where it always started.

Mama and Daddy were gazing at each other. Slowly their eyes moved to her.

"You were right," Sophie said. "This is too much for sixth graders. It's messed everything up, and I don't want to have anything to do with it."

"All right," Daddy said, "who are you, and what have you done with Sophie?"

Mama gave him a hard jab with her elbow and looked at Sophie with a shine in her eyes. "We're proud of you, Dream Girl. And I'm still going to finish that dress."

Sophie wasn't sure she could stick to her decision if she saw that gorgeous piece of gold and lace, much less put it on. And there were even harder things than that to face now—like Fiona—and Darbie—and Kitty.

First thing tomorrow before school, before we even practice, she decided.

And then she talked to Jesus some more.

Twelve

By the time she finished her homework, Sophie had a plan. She was nervous, but, as she told herself, "I have to get this out of the way." She took a deep breath and called Maggie.

Senora LaQuita told her she didn't think Maggie would come to the phone.

"Please—just ask her?" Sophie said. Her voice was barely squeaking out.

Sophie heard Maggie's mom call out something in Spanish—twice—three times—until finally a frail voice said, "Hello?" sounding more like a pin-drop than a thud.

"Maggie?" Sophie said.

"I'm only taking the phone because my mom is making me," Maggie said.

Sophie's hand tightened around the phone until her fingers went white. "I just want to say, please come to school tomorrow. I'll protect you—I promise."

There was a heavy silence. Then Maggie's words dropped with close to their usual clunk. "I don't care if I ever go back to that school again—but my mom's making me do that too."

"Meet us on the playground early, okay?" Sophie held her breath again.

"Whatever," Maggie said. And then she hung up.

Love is where it starts, Sophie reminded herself. *I sure hope Dr. Peter is right.*

When Mama dropped Sophie off at school—earlier than the bus—the next morning, Darbie and Fiona were waiting for her on the sidewalk, and they half dragged her to their spot backstage.

"Are we glad to see you!" Fiona said as she finally let go of Sophie under the flower arch.

"We thought you'd still be mad at us after yesterday," Darbie said.

Fiona hooked her elbow around Sophie's neck. "I wish we hadn't had that fight—especially since the dance is going to happen anyway."

Darbie nodded soberly. "You can't help what your mum and dad do."

"I'm not going," Sophie said.

She could feel Fiona's arm going stiff around her neck.

"You're not going to the dance?" Fiona said.

"Aunt Emily said I can go," Darbie said. "I just can't dance with only Ian the whole night." She shook her head. "Sophie, your parents really ARE strict."

"They didn't tell me I couldn't go. I decided myself."

Fiona let go of her completely. "WHAT?" she said. "But what about your dress?"

"I can use the dress in our film."

"What about Jimmy?"

"I'll just tell him the truth: the whole thing is messed up, and Maggie doesn't want to be my friend now because of it, and maybe Kitty either."

Sophie lowered her eyes. She'd said what she knew was right to say, but she didn't want to hear what Fiona and Darbie were going to say back. Maybe if she didn't look at them, the words wouldn't come out of their mouths.

"Sophie! You guys! You gotta come right now!"

Sophie turned around in time to see Willoughby burst through the curtains in a billow of dust.

"Why?" Fiona said. "If this is some kind of trick—"

"They've got Maggie on the playground—she needs you. Come on!"

Without asking who "they" were, Sophie charged off the stage, through the cafeteria, and out the back door. Darbie and Fiona were right behind her.

"I told Maggie to meet us out here!" Sophie cried. "I told her we'd protect her!"

"We'll take care of those Corn Pops!" Fiona said.

Willoughby ran ahead and led them around the corner of the school to the area where the trash Dumpsters stood. At first Sophie didn't see anyone, until Willoughby stopped and motioned for them to look between two of the giant green boxes. It wasn't the Corn Pops they saw. It was the Fruit Loops.

Tod was sitting on top of one of the boxes, dangling his legs as he looked down. Colton had his back to them, facing Eddie, intent on doing something that obviously cracked up the other two. Their faces were exploding with hysterical laughter. When Fiona yanked Colton back by his shirt, Sophie saw why.

There was Maggie, with Eddie's arms wrapped across her chest from behind, and she had what looked like a donut stuffed halfway into her mouth. It was hard to tell which was bulging more, her cheeks or her eyes, as she coughed and choked.

Colton held a Krispy Kreme box over his head as he stumbled into Darbie. Fiona made a dive to catch her before she careened into the side of the Dumpster, Sophie hurled herself straight at Eddie, and Maggie and hung with her whole weight on Eddie's arm.

"Dude!" he shouted.

He let go of Maggie, but before Sophie could even reach for her, she felt her own arms being pulled behind her back. It wasn't Colton who was doing it. It was B.J.

"Get off me, you little *eejit*," Darbie cried—because Anne-Stuart had leaped onto her back like a spider monkey.

Fiona had both hands entwined with Julia's, pushing her back, obviously to keep from being slashed by her fingernails. As Sophie watched in horror, Julia spit into Fiona's face.

But that wasn't the worst of it. Maggie was on her hands and knees, spewing out pieces of donut and rocking as if she were going to throw up any second. Sophie took two steps toward her and ran smack into Tod—who had apparently come down from on high.

"Going somewhere?" he said. His whole face seemed to come to a point just inches from hers. And then it was gone as he twisted her around, latched his arms around her, and picked her up. "Dude, we gotta get rid of the garbage around here. It's starting to smell."

Eddie was up against the dumpster with Colton standing on his shoulders. Tod plunked Sophie into Eddie's arms, and Eddie lifted her up to Colton as if she were one of the donuts.

"Watch this!" Colton said. He flipped Sophie over and held her upside down. There was no decision to be made about what to do—screams ripped out of her and she banged her fists against anything close enough to reach.

Sophie looked around frantically as her head began to throb. Even upside-down she could see B.J. with Fiona in a headlock, and Anne-Stuart and Julia sitting on Darbie while she clawed at the air and shrieked about eejits. Both her Corn Flakes were putting up a good fight, but the Corn Pops weren't giving in—and Sophie felt herself being hoisted, head still lolling, toward the opening to the Dumpster. Willoughby was nowhere in sight.

"Somebody HELP!" Sophie screamed.

"Wythe here," said a voice above her. "JAMES Wythe."

Sophie curled upward. Jimmy's head appeared above the dumpster, and then his whole chest appeared as he pulled himself up by his gymnast-muscled arms and swung the rest of his body over the side. He dropped past Sophie to the ground and yelled, "Ready, Double-O-Nine?"

Another head popped out of the Dumpster—Vincent's this time—and he reached out and grabbed one of Colton's ears. "Drop her," he said.

"Dude! Let go!"

"Not until you drop her!"

"Don't drop me!" Sophie screamed.

But Colton did, right into Jimmy's arms. He set her down almost as soon as she realized where she was and moved in front of her. Vincent was now sitting on Colton's shoulders, fingers wrapped around both of Colton's ears.

"One move and I pull," Vincent said.

By now Eddie's face resembled a turnip, and he hurled himself at Jimmy. But Jimmy stepped aside, taking Sophie with him, just in time to avoid being plowed down by Eddie's chunk of a body plummeting to the ground.

"What the—" she heard Tod shout, sounding as if he were inside a cave.

Sophie peered around Jimmy. *Make that a bag*, she thought. Ian and Ross were wrapping Tod soundly inside a large cloth sack with a hunk of yellow rope from the bottom of the Dumpster.

"Eddie—get up and do something!" Colton cried, voice cracking.

"I can't!" Eddie said.

It was easy to see why. His ankles were tied together with more yellow rope. Nathan appeared from the other side, dusting off his hands and grinning like he'd just taken a gold medal.

"Good work Double-O-Eleven," Jimmy said. "What is the status of Agent Canary?"

Nathan whipped something black out of his pocket and talked into it. "Canary, this is Double-O-Eleven. Do you read me?"

"Canary?" Fiona said.

Sophie stepped all the way out from behind Jimmy. Fiona was rubbing her neck—and B.J. was long gone. So were Julia and Anne-Stuart. Darbie was frozen in an I'm-going-after-them position, staring at Jimmy.

"Are you talking about Kitty?" she said.

"Canary has the spies in her sights," Nathan said as he returned what was obviously a walkie-talkie to his pocket. "She and Mockingbird will keep a tail on them until help arrives. She'll advise if they head back this way."

"Who's Mockingbird?" Darbie said.

"I don't know," Nathan said. "I thought you did."

Sophie didn't catch the rest of the discussion. She went to Maggie, who was still on her knees, wiping her mouth with the back of her shaking hand.

"Did you throw up?" Sophie whispered to her.

Maggie shook her head. "None of it went down. I spit it all out. They said I would never get skinny—that I was always feeding my cake trap anyway, so they were going to 'help' me."

Sophie knelt down beside her. "I let you down again. I'm really sorry—"

117

There was no answer. Maggie spit another sugary glob into the dirt.

"Do you hate me now?" Sophie said. "You probably do — but Maggie, I LOVE you, and I'll never hurt you ever again. I'm not even going to the stupid dance."

"Me neither," said a voice above them.

"I wouldn't go if they PAID me," said another one.

Sophie's head came up. Fiona and Darbie were standing over them. Their faces looked ready to crumple.

Nathan's walkie-talkie crackled, and he pawed it out of his pocket. "Double-O-Eleven here. Come in, Canary."

There was more sputtering that Sophie couldn't make out, but it brought a grin to Nathan's — Double-O-Eleven's — face.

"She said the Corn Pops were on their way back here, but Mockingbird and two other agents cornered them at the door." Nathan's eyes crunched up. "Some kind of cereal?"

"Wheaties?" Sophie said.

"Yeah, that was it. Canary has gone to get O."

"O?" Fiona said. "Oh! Mrs. Olinghouse!"

"Are you talking about Kitty?" Darbie said to Nathan. "OUR Kitty?"

While Nathan's ears went so red they looked like Christmas lights, Sophie turned her attention back to Maggie.

"I'm going to protect you," Sophie said. "Even if you hate me — "

"I don't hate you." Maggie sank back and folded her arms around her knees so she could hug them against her. "But you can't be around me to protect me every minute. And people are always going to do stuff like that to me. I'm never gonna be skinny — I'm not made that way, and somebody's always gonna say I'm fat."

"Those guys are slime," Jimmy said.

Jimmy squatted down in front of the Corn Flakes, looking suddenly as if he didn't know where to put the arms that could, as far as Sophie was concerned, do just about anything.

"You aren't fat and besides, even if you were—" Jimmy swallowed, so that Sophie could see his Adam's apple bobbing up and down. "—you don't deserve to be treated like that."

Vincent gave Colton's head a shake. "Whenever you need assistance, Agent Owl, just call on us."

"How did you know her code name was Owl?" Fiona said.

"Canary told us," Nathan said. "When SHE came to me for protection."

"From what?" Darbie said.

"From the Corn Pops. They threatened her with bodily harm if she got in the way of these morons. Mockingbird told her this was going to go down, but she couldn't tell YOU agents because the Corn Pops' threat covered you all too."

It was the most Sophie had ever heard Nathan say. He must have realized it too, because his ears turned into Christmas bulbs again.

"WHO is Mockingbird?" Darbie said.

But she didn't get an answer, because "O" rounded the corner of the Dumpster with Mr. Denton and Kitty.

"All right, guys, turn them loose," Mr. Denton said.

"They were saving us from being thrown into the garbage!" Sophie said.

Mr. Denton took a sniff at Vincent. "You really got into it, didn't you? Okay—let's go sort this out."

He nodded for Colton to come with him and waited while Nathan untied Eddie—who had been lying facedown ever since he'd fallen. Sophie could see that he'd been spending the time crying.

"Where's the other one?" Mr. Denton said.

Ian and Ross whipped the bag off Tod. Sophie wasn't sure, but she thought a hint of a smile trailed across Mr. Denton's face.

When they were gone, along with Jimmy, Nathan, Vincent, and the twins, Mrs. Olinghouse turned to the Corn Flakes.

"I want you to tell me the absolute, unvarnished truth about how Julia and B.J. and Anne-Stuart were involved in this."

"You can count on us," Fiona said. "Especially Sophie. She's always honest."

"If your story matches Kitty's and Willoughby's," Mrs. Olinghouse said, "then I think Julia and her friends are in a great deal of trouble. They've had enough chances this year."

"Excuse me," Sophie said. "Did you say Willoughby?"

"Yes, ma'am, Willoughby Wiley. I just talked to her and Kitty. I was surprised she would turn her friends in, and I thought maybe they'd had a falling-out and this was her revenge." She turned her sharp blue eyes on Sophie. "But if you confirm it, I guess I'd better believe it, hadn't I?"

"Willoughby is Mockingbird," Fiona whispered to Darbie and Sophie as they followed "O" into the building. "I'm going to have to get down on my KNEES to apologize to her."

"I know," Sophie whispered back.

"Ahem," Darbie said. She was grinning. "A lady does not whisper."

And Mrs. Olinghouse made it clear that a lady does not threaten or conspire or hold people against their will either. The Corn Pops were suspended for five days.

Except for Willoughby, who made it official when she sat with the Corn Flakes at lunch that day, that she was no longer one of Julia's Pops.

"I think you should be one of us," Kitty said. Then she glanced quickly at the other Corn Flakes. "I mean, if that's okay."

They all looked at one another and nodded, except for Maggie, who was tearing the roll from her sandwich into pieces and not eating it.

"Is it all right with you, Mags?" Sophie said.

"Do I still get a vote?" she said.

"Well, duh-uh—you're a Corn Flake!" Fiona said.

"I don't know if I fit in so much anymore." Maggie let the last chunk of bread drop into her lunch box. "You all have boys liking you—and you're pretty—and you look good in clothes. I'm never gonna have any of that."

"That's a bit of a horse's hoof, I think!" Darbie said.

Maggie looked at Darbie with hopeless eyes. "You wouldn't say that if you were more like me. Any of you."

"But we ARE like you!" Kitty said.

"We're all alike in the important things," Sophie said.

"Yes!" Darbie pulled her eyebrows together. "Tell us what they are, Sophie."

Sophie got up on her knees so she could look right into Maggie's dark, sad eyes. "None of us are perfect," she said. "But we ALL try to follow our rules—like we're all mostly loyal and we don't do bad stuff to people like the Corn Pops even though they do it to us—and we TRY to do the right thing. When we fight, we always make up because—"

Sophie stopped and slid her eyes toward Kitty—whose parents "didn't believe in church." She was pretty sure Jesus would want her to go ahead anyway.

"Because what?" Kitty said.

"Because love is always where it starts with God."

Willoughby stuck her hand up. "If you call Julia and them Corn Pops," she said, "what do you call yourselves?"

Darbie and Fiona and Kitty whipped their heads toward Sophie.

121

"Willoughby totally helped us," Sophie said. "Of course we can tell her. We're the Corn Flakes."

Willoughby gave a nod that bounced her wavy bob. "Then I want to be one."

Fiona looked at Maggie. "Mags?" she said.

"Yeah," Maggie thudded.

Sophie suddenly felt a little squirmy. "Just one thing," she said to Willoughby. "We're not like some clique. I mean, we have other friends too."

Willoughby looked down the table at Gill and Harley.

"Yeah," Darbie said. "The Wheaties."

"And don't forget the Lucky Charms," Sophie said.

Question marks formed in Corn Flake eyes, until Fiona said, "OH—Jimmy and those guys. But I thought we said no boyfriends."

"They aren't boyfriends," Sophie said. "They're boys who are friends. I think it's our time for that."

"Yes!" Kitty said. "They are our Lucky Charms!" She high-fived Sophie and Darbie and Fiona. And then even Maggie put up her hand and let Kitty slap it—about fifteen times.

Dr. Peter WAS right, Sophie thought. *Love IS always where it starts with God.*

They got word later that day from Willoughby, who just seemed to know everything that happened at Great Marsh Elementary, that the Fruit Loops were suspended for the rest of the year. And the dance was cancelled.

"There isn't going to be a dance after all," Sophie told her parents when Daddy got home that night. "I figure you're happy to know that."

They seemed more than just happy. They looked the way they did when everybody finally woke up on Christmas morning.

"We have a surprise," Mama said.

Sophie looked back and forth between them. Daddy was sporting a major grin.

"You wanted a dance," he said, "so you're going to have one—you and the rest of the Corn Flakes."

"At Fiona's house," Mama said. "It's being decorated as we speak."

Daddy nudged Mama. "Don't tell her everything!"

"I'm excited!" Mama said. She was all but clapping her little elfin hands. "Your dress is upstairs, all finished. You need to go get into it—your date will be waiting."

"My date?" Sophie said. "But I thought—"

Mama nodded at Daddy, who was holding up his hand. "Will I do?" he said.

"Are all the dads—?"

"Yes," Mama said.

"And Darbie's uncle Patrick?"

"Yes."

"But what about Maggie?"

"Boppa to the rescue," Daddy said. "IF she can get him away from Miss Odetta."

"Of course she can," Mama said. "This whole thing was Miss Odetta's idea."

"No WAY!" Sophie said.

"There's only one problem." Daddy shuffled his feet. "I'm not a dancer."

Sophie felt a grin spreading across her face. "That's not a problem. I can teach you." She put her arms out. "We'll start with a waltz."

Daddy lifted her so her feet were on his and leaned down to get into position.

"It's one-two-three, one-two-three," Sophie said, and they began to move.

"I want to be the most important guy in your life for a while longer, Soph," Daddy said in a soft voice she didn't even know he had.

"You are, Daddy," Sophie said.

And then she thought, *You and Jesus.*

With that, Sophie decided not to think of a new mission, now that the old one had been accomplished. She just swept across the kitchen, dancing with her daddy.

Glossary

a.k.a. (ay-kay-ay) a cool way of saying "also known as"

accommodate (a-KAH-mah-date) make room for something

alter (ALL-ter) to fix or change a piece of clothing so it fits better

astonishingly (a-STOHN-ish-ing-lee) a word that describes something done so incredibly well that people can't help but be amazed

blackguards (BLAG-ghards) very rude and offensive people

class (klas) not a group of students, but a word that means something's really cool

demerit (di-MARE-it) kind of like traffic tickets for your behavior; if you get too many of them, you are punished

disdainful (dis-DANE-full) when you think you're better than someone else, and look at them with so much disgust that you show your feelings on your face

enchanting (in-CHANT-ing) something that is so charming and fantastic that it casts a spell on you

flagellating (FLA-gel-late-ing) constantly bringing up something you did wrong to punish yourself; kind of like beating yourself up

flick (flik) a fun word for "movie"

foil (foyl) to keep something from happening, usually through some sort of plan

formidable (for-MI-da-bull) a problem so big and scary that there doesn't seem to be any way to avoid or defeat it

inconsiderate (in-kon-SI-dehr-ret) not thinking about other people, and doing what you want instead

irresponsible (ir-e-spahn-se-bule) not doing the things you're supposed to do, such as chores, coming home on time, or your homework

keening (keyn-ing) crying really loud, like when someone dies

nostalgic (na-STALL-jick) something old that makes you all mushy inside, so that you want to live in the time period it's from

resilient (re-zill-yent) someone who is really tough, and can bounce back quickly from difficult things

scandalized (SKAN-duhl-eyzed) what happens after people are totally shocked by something. Sometimes, these people are very mean to the person who is "shocking," and spread gossip about them.

scornful (scorn-full) hateful, in a I'm-better-than-you way, and making sure people know how you feel

steely (STEE-lee) to look at someone in a cold way, like when you're disappointed in them

succumb (suh-come) when you finally give into something more powerful than you

surveillance (sir-VAY-lents) to secretly follow and spy on someone closely in order to gather special information on that person

Victorian (vic-TORE-ee-an) literally something that was made during the reign of Queen Victoria (1837 – 1901), when everything was really fancy. Victorian homes in America are usually pastel, and have a lot of fancy stuff on the outside.

Introduce your mom to Nancy Rue!

Today's mom is raising her 8-to-12-year-old daughter in a society that compels her little girl to grow up too fast. *Moms' Ultimate Guide to the Tween Girl World* gives mothe practical advice and spiritual inspiration to guide their mini-women into adolescence as strong, confident, authentic, an God-centered young women; even in a morally challenged society and without losing the childhoods before they're read